GREAT SCIENTISTS

KNOW ABOUT THE LIFE OF GENIUSES

Dr. Gagan Jain, *D.Litt.*

NEW DELHI (INDIA)

GREAT SCIENTISTS

KNOW ABOUT THE LIFE OF GENIUSES

This English Edition, Published in India

Published by

MG BOOKS

An Imprint of

MAANU GRAPHICS

(PUBLISHERS OF GENERAL BOOKS)

5FF, Ganpati Bhawan, 21 Ansari Road,
Darya Ganj, New Delhi-110002
Ph: 43755225, 9315898404
E-mail : maanugraphics@yahoo.com
mgbooks.maanu@yahoo.com

Printed at

Satyam Enterprises, Delhi

CONTENTS

ALBERT EINSTEIN

Albert Einstein was born into a Jewish family and had a lifelong respect for his Jewish heritage. Around the time Einstein was eleven years old he went through an intense religious phase, during which time he followed Jewish religious precepts in detail, including abstaining from eating pork. During this time he composed several songs in honor of God. But during most of his life Einstein was not a practicing Jew.

Einstein was opposed to atheism. Various sources refer to him as a mostly non-practicing Jew, an agnostic, or simply as a person with an idiosyncratic personal worldview.

Einstein's Jewish background and upbringing were significant to him, and his Jewish identity was strong, increasingly so as he grew older. The simple appellation "agnostic" may not be entirely accurate, given his many expressions of belief in a Spinozan concept of Deity. Certainly the adult Einstein was not a kosher-keeping, synagogue-attending traditional adherent of Judaism. But it is accurate enough to call his religious affiliation "Jewish," with the understanding of the variety encompassed by such a label.

Although Einstein had a positive attitude toward religion, he was not active during adulthood in any organized religious group. It seems that as an adult he was only once a dues-paying member of a Jewish congregation.

Most sources indicate that he clearly did not believe in a personal God, and that when he talked about God he was speaking in a more Spinozan sense, and was not speaking of a strictly Judeo-Christian Biblical conception of God.

He wrote of his belief in a noble "cosmic religious feeling" that enables scientists to advance human knowledge. One of Einstein's most famous quotes on the subject of science and religion is: "Science without religion is lame, religion without science is blind."

Einstein is said to have held a concept of God similar to that promulgated by Jewish philosopher Baruch Spinoza. Einstein studied Spinoza and identified with Spinoza both culturally and philosophically.

The Encyclopedia Britannica says of him: "Firmly denying atheism, Einstein expressed a belief in 'Spinoza's God who reveals himself in the harmony of what exists.' This actually motivated his interest in science, as he once remarked to a young physicist: 'I want to know how God created this world, I am not interested in this or that phenomenon, in the spectrum of this or that element. I want to know His thoughts, the rest are details.' Einstein's famous epithet on the 'uncertainty principle' was 'God does not play dice.'"

It has been reported by some Christian Science sources that Einstein attended Christian Science services in New York and that Einstein said that Mary Baker Eddy was right in her theories about an essentially non-physical universe. We have no expertise on the Einstein-Christian Science connection and it is beyond the scope of this page to analyze the subject in detail, but we mention this for the sake of completeness.

Given Einstein's political views and penchant for peace activism, it is not surprising that he also expressed fondness for and appreciation for the Quakers, a Christian denominational family more formally known as the Religious Society of Friends. In a letter to A. Chapple of Australia (23 February 1954), Einstein said: "I consider the Society of Friends the religious community which has the highest moral standards. As far as I know, they have never made evil compromises and are always guided by their conscience. In international life, especially, their influence seems to me very beneficial and effective."

Einstein said ("Einstein, Albert" in *The Enlightened Mind*, ed. Stephen Mitchell; New York: Harper Collins, 1991): The most beautiful and profound emotion we can experience is the sensation of the mystical. It is the source of all true science. He to whom this emotion is a stranger, who can no longer wonder and stand rapt in awe, is as good as dead. To know that what is impenetrable to us really exists, manifesting itself as the highest wisdom and the most radiant beauty, which our dull faculties can comprehend only in their primitive forms — this knowledge, this feeling, is at the center of true religion.

In a letter to V. T. Aaltonen (7 May 1952), Einstein explained his opinion that belief in a personal God is better than atheism. Einstein said, "Mere unbelief in a personal God is no philosophy at all." In a letter to Hans Muehsam (30 March 1954), Einstein said: "I am a deeply religious nonbeliever... This is a somewhat new kind of religion."

In a letter to a child who asked if scientists pray (24 January 1936), said: "Everyone who is seriously involved in the pursuit of science becomes convinced that a spirit is manifest in the laws of the Universe - a spirit vastly superior to that of man... In this way the pursuit of science leads to a religious feeling of a special sort, which is indeed quite different from the religiosity of someone more naive."

In a letter to M. Berkowitz (25 October 1950), Einstein said: "My position concerning God is that of an agnostic. I am convinced that a vivid consciousness of the primary importance of moral principles for the betterment and ennoblement of life does not need the idea of a law-giver, especially a law-giver who works on the basis of reward and punishment."

In a letter to an Iowa student who asked, What is God? (July 1953), Einstein said, "To assume the existence of an unperceivable being... does not facilitate understanding the orderliness we find in the perceivable world."

ALESSANDRO VOLTA

Volta, Alessandro, Count, Italian physicist, known for his pioneering work in electricity, invented the Electric Battery in 1800. Volta was born in Como and educated in the public schools there. In 1774 he became professor of physics at the Royal School in Como, and in the following year he devised the electrophorus, an instrument that produced charges of static electricity. In 1776-77 he applied himself to chemistry, studying atmospheric electricity and devising experiments such as the ignition of gases by an electric spark in a closed vessel. In 1779 he became professor of physics at the University of Pavia, a chair he occupied for 25 years.

By 1800 he had developed the so-called voltaic pile, a forerunner of the electric battery, which produced a steady stream of electricity. In honor of his work in the field of electricity, Napoleon made him a count in 1801. The electrical unit known as the volt was named in his honor. In 1819 he finally retired to private life in his country house in Camnago, where he died in 1827.

In 1800, he announced a new electrical device, the Voltaic Pile, initially presented as an "artificial electric organ", in controversy with the claimed autonomy of animal electricity. This device was made of alternating disks of zinc and copper with each pair separated by brine soaked cloth. Attaching a wire to either end produces a continuous current of low intensity.

This was the first direct current battery. This put an end (for a time) to Galvani's theory of animal electricity. It is interesting to note that Volta described his battery as an electric organ and likened it to the electric organ of the torpedo fish, which had columnar stacks of cells.

The importance of the invention and its applications, which came about in a few months, seemed to prove the Como scientist right. His fame has since conquered the world. But the idea of animal electricity did not prove useless. Volta's invention was to give rise to electrochemistry, electromagnetism and the modern applications of electricity.

Galvani's research was soon to develop into electrophysiology and modern biology. The possibility of producing electric currents was to change science and technology in the new century.

As an experimental physicist and inventor of instruments, Volta enjoyed unequaled success, but nowadays one must remember also his notable theoretical contributions (the product of intensive and extensive quantities, tension, capacity, the law of bimetallic contact, atmospheric electricity) which, while going against the Newtonian line, were to prove invaluable for the development of the experimental sciences of the eighteenth century.

Volta received his greatest honor at the hands of his fellow scientists. The unit of electromotive force- the driving force that moves the electric current- is now called the "volt." The energy of moving charged particles produced by modern atom-smashing machines is measured in electron-volts.

A billion electron-volts is abbreviated "bev," and when we speak of the particular atom-smasher called the bevatron, the "v" in the name stands for Volta.

ALEXANDER GRAHAM BELL

Alexander Graham Bell (March 3, 1847 - August 2, 1922) was a scientist, inventor, and founder of the Bell telephone company. In addition to his work in telecommunications technology, he also was responsible for important advances in aviation and hydrofoil technology.

Bell was born in Edinburgh, Scotland. He came of a family associated with the teaching of elocution: his grandfather in London, his uncle in Dublin, and his father, Mr. Alexander Melville Bell, in Edinburgh, were all professed elocutionists.

The latter has published a variety of works on the subject, several of which are well known, especially his treatise on Visible Speech, which appeared in Edinburgh in 1868. In this he explains his ingenious method of instructing deaf mutes, by means of their eyesight, how to articulate words, and also how to read what other persons are saying by the motions of their lips. Graham Bell, his distinguished son, was educated at the Royal High School of

Edinburgh, from which he graduated at the age of thirteen. At the age of sixteen he secured a position as a pupil-teacher of elocution and music in Weston House Academy, at Elgin in Morayshire. The next year he spent at the University of Edinburgh. From 1866 to 1867 he was an instructor at Somersetshire College at Bath, England. While still in Scotland he is said to have turned his attention to the science of acoustics, with a view to ameliorate the deafness of his mother.

In 1870 he moved with his family to Canada where they settled at Brantford, Ontario. Before he left Scotland, Alexander Graham Bell had turned his attention to telephony, and in Canada he continued an interest in communication machines. He designed a piano which could transmit its music to a distance by means of electricity. In 1873 he accompanied his father to Montreal, Quebec, where he was employed in teaching the system of visible speech.

The elder Bell was invited to introduce the system into a large day-school for mutes at Boston, but he declined the post in favour of his son, who soon became famous in the United States for his success in this important work. Alexander Graham Bell published more than one treatise on the subject at Washington, and it is mainly through his efforts that thousands of deaf mutes in America are now able to speak almost, if not quite, as well as persons who are able to hear.

At Boston he continued his researches in the same field, and endeavoured to produce a telephone which would not only send musical notes, but articulate speech. With financing from his American father-in-law, on March 7, 1876, the U.S. Patent Office granted him Patent Number 174,465 covering "the method of, and apparatus for, transmitting vocal or other sounds telegraphically . . . by causing electrical undulations, similar in form to the vibrations of the air accompanying the said vocal or other sound.", the telephone. (It should be noted that the question of who invented the telephone continues to be debated.

It is clear that several people were researching similar devices. However, supporters of Bell claim that his was the first fully working design.

After obtaining the patent for the telephone, Bell continued his experiments in communication, which culminated in the invention of the photophone-transmission of sound on a beam of light — a precursor of today's optical fiber systems. He also worked in medical research and invented techniques for teaching speech to the deaf. The range of Bell's inventive genius is represented only in part by the 18 patents granted in his name alone and the 12 he shared with his collaborators.

These included 14 for the telephone and telegraph, four for the photophone, one for the phonograph, five for aerial vehicles, four for hydroairplanes, and two for a selenium cell. In 1888 he was one of the founding members of the National Geographic Society and became its second president. He was the recipient of many honors. The French Government conferred on him the decoration of the Légion d'honneur (Legion of Honor), the Académie française bestowed on him the Volta Prize of 50,000 Francs, the Royal Society of Arts in London awarded him the Albert medal in 1902, and the University of Würzburg, Bavaria, granted him the Degree of Ph.D. Bell married Mabel Hubbard on July 11, 1877. He died in Baddeck, Nova Scotia in 1922.

In 2004, Alexander Graham Bell was nominated as one of the top 10 "Greatest Canadians" by viewers of the Canadian Broadcasting Corporation.

ALFRED NOBEL

Alfred Nobel was born the son of a Swedish construction worker in Stockholm, 1833. His father, Immanuel, often built bridges, and so was interested in finding different ways to blast away unwanted rock formations.

In the year of Alfred's birth however, the construction business went bankrupt. Seeing nothing left for him in Sweden, Immanuel and his family moved to St. Petersburg in Russia, where a factory was set up, making mines out of gunpowder, for use by the Russian Army during the Crimean War. The demand for this product was high, the business was booming and Alfred Nobel and the other children received an excellent private education whilst in Russia. His father also insisted that he travel the world during his education, and by the age of seventeen, he was fluent in five different languages.

Having been educated in chemical engineering, Alfred Nobel returned to St. Petersburg to try and develop a safe way of handling the highly volatile liquid nitro-glycerine, which had recently been invented. The family were forced to return to Stockholm though before any real progress was made – the end of the Crimean War also meant the end of the mine making business.

Back in Sweden, an explosion involving nitro-glycerine resulted in the death of his brother, convincing Alfred that a safer alternative must be developed. Eventually, he discovered that by mixing nitro-glycerine with silica, the end product could be moulded into cylinder shapes, and was not greatly affected by minor fluctuations in temperature and pressure. In 1867 he patented the product, calling it dynamite.

It was five times more powerful than ordinary gunpowder, and so very quickly became a sought after commodity in the world of mining and construction. Dynamite was used the world over, for work such as blasting the Alpine Tunnel on the St. Gotthard rail line and cutting the Corinth Canal in Greece.

Within a few years, Alfred Nobel had increased the production of dynamite from his factories dramatically, and showed his supreme skill as a businessman by being able to sell it all over the world. Although to a certain extent the product sold itself due to its effectiveness, the organisation shown in the production and distribution of huge amounts of dynamite are a credit to his entrepreneurial efforts.

Although he worked for the majority of his life developing explosives, Nobel was essentially a pacifist. When, in his later years he drew up a will, he stated that he wished the majority of his nine million dollar fortune to be used to fund awards in different fields of study (Physics, Chemistry, Literature, Physiology and Medicine, Peace). He stated that the awards should be given to 'those who have conferred the greatest benefit to mankind'.

It was five years after his death that the first Nobel awards were handed out, in 1901. The Nobel foundation had been set up to organise and structure the awards. Since their inception the Nobel prizes have come to be recognised as the highest honour a person can recieve in a particular area of study.

Although Alfred Nobel made an important discovery as a scientist, that of dynamite, and used his powers as an industrialist to produce and then sell the product, he should be best remembered for his legacy. Through his will, outstanding artists, scientists and humanitarians alike have been able to push through their invaluable work for the good of humankind.

A. P. J. ABDUL KALAM

Born on 15th October 1931 at Rameswaram, in Tamil Nadu, Dr. Avul Pakir Jainulabdeen Abdul Kalam, specialized in Aero Engineering from Madras Institute of Technology. He initially worked in DRDO in 1958 and then joined ISRO in 1963. Dr. Kalam has made significant contribution to Indian satellite and launch vehicles of ISRO and also in the missile programme of DRDO. As project Director, SLV-III, he contributed for the design, development and management of India's first indigenous Satellite Launch Vehicle (SLV-III) to inject Rohini satellite in the near earth orbit. He was responsible for the evolution of ISRO's launch vehicles programme and configurations. He rejoined DRDO in 1982 and conceived the Integrated Guided Missile Development Programme (IGMDP) for indigenous missiles.

Kalam was born in a middle-class family in Rameshwaram, Tamilnadu, a town well-known for its Hindu shrines. His mother tongue is Tamil. His father, a devout Muslim, owned boats which he rented out to local fishermen and was a good friend of Hindu religious leaders and the school teachers at Rameshwaram. APJ Abdul Kalam mentions in his biography that to support his studies, he started his career as a newspaper vendor. This was also told in the book, *A Boy and His Dream: Three Stories from the Childhood of Abdul Kalam* by Vinita Krishna. The house Kalam was born in can still be found on the Mosque street at Rameswaram, and his brother's curio shop abuts it. This has become a point-of-call for tourists who seek out the place. Kalam grew up in an intimate relationship with nature, and he says in *Wings of Fire* that he never could imagine that water could be so powerful a destroying force as that he witnessed when he was six. That was in 1934 when a cyclonic storm swept away the Pamban bridge and a trainload of passengers with it and also Kalam's native village, Dhanushkodi.

Kalam observes strict personal discipline, vegetarianism, teetotalism and celibacy. Kalam is a scholar of Thirukkural; in most of his speeches, he quotes at least one *kural.* Kalam has written several inspirational books, most notably his autobiography *Wings of Fire*, aimed at motivating Indian youth. Another of his books, *Guiding Souls: Dialogues on the Purpose of Life* reveals his spiritual side. He has written poems in Tamil as well. It has been reported that there is considerable demand in South Korea for translated versions of books authored by him.

Dr. Kalam visited the Carnegie Mellon campus on October 16th, 2007 where he spoke in front of numerous students and faculty regarding the role of science and the view of India in the future. He received a honorary doctorate from the university.

He was Scientific Adviser to Defence Minister and Secretary, Department of Defence Research & Development from July 1992 to December 1999.As Chairman, Technology Information, Forecasting and Assessment Council (TIFAC), he generated the Technology Vision 2020 documents – a road map for transforming India from Developing India to Developed India. He provided overall guidance to a number of Homegrown Technology Projects and major technology missions such as Sugar, Advanced Composites and Fly Ash utilization. Dr. Kalam has served as the Principal Scientific Advisor to the Government of

India, in the rank of Cabinet Minister, from November 1999 to November 2001. He was primarily responsible for evolving policies, strategies and missions for generation of innovations and support systems for multiple applications. Also, generating science and technology task in strategic, economic and social sectors in partnership with Government departments, institutions and industry.

Dr. Kalam was also the Chairman, Ex-officio, of the Scientific Advisory Committee to the Cabinet (SAC-C). Dr. Kalam took up academic pursuit as Professor, Technology & Societal Transformation at Anna University, Chennai and involved in teaching and research tasks. Above all he is on his mission to ignite the young minds for national development by meeting high school students across the country.

Dr. Kalam was conferred with the Degree of Doctor of Science (D.Sc. Honoris Causa) by 30 universities/academic institutions. He is recipient of several awards including the Indira Gandhi Award for National Integration 1997.Dr. A.P.J. Abdul Kalam has been awarded Padma Bhushan in 1981, Padma Vibhushan in 1990 and BHARAT RATNA in 1997.

While delivering a lecture at the Indian Institute of Management Shillong, Kalam collapsed and died from an apparent cardiac arrest on 27 July 2015, aged 83. Thousands including national-level dignitaries attended the funeral ceremony held in his hometown of Rameshwaram, where he was buried with full state honours

ARCHIMEDES

Archimedes was born in the Greek city of Syracuse, on the island of Sicily, in 287 B.C. He was the son of Phidias, the astronomer and mathematician. What we know of Archimedes' life comes from his extant writings, and from the histories authored by Plutarch, Cicero, and other historians several centuries after his death. Due to the length of time between Archimedes' death and his biographers' accounts, as well as inconsistencies among their writings, details of his life must remain subject to question.

Plutarch records that Archimedes was a relative of King Hieron, but Cicero claims he was of low birth. It is believed he obtained his early schooling in Syracuse, then traveled to Alexandria to study with Conon, the Egyptian mathematician and astronomer. Archimedes was close friends with both Conon and the custodian of the Alexandrian library, Eratosthenes. He corresponded with them about his mathematical and scientific discoveries long after he had completed his formal studies and returned to Syracuse.

Archimedes' contributions to mathematical knowledge were diverse. On the subject of plane geometry three of the treatises he wrote have survived, *Measurement of a Circle*, *Quadrature of the Parabola*, and *On Spirals*. In *Measurement of a Circle*, he described his method for calculating , the ratio between the circumference of a circle and its diameter. By a method that involved measuring the perimeter of inscribed and circumscribed polygons, Archimedes correctly determined that the value of was somewhere between 3.1408 and 3.1428.

In the same treatise he set forth the formula r^2 for determining a circle's area. In *Quadrature of the Parabola*and *On Spirals*, Archimedes advanced his technique for determining the area under curves, a sophisticated version of the method of exhaustion, originally developed by the Egyptians. His use of this technique, elaborated upon in another volume, The *Method*, anticipated the development of integral calculus by two thousand years.

Archimedes dealt with the topic of solid geometry in his writings *On the Sphere and Cylinder*and *On Conoids and Spheroids*. *On the Sphere and Cylinder* contains several famous proofs, including his demonstration that the volume of a sphere is equal to $4/3\ r^3$. Archimedes also showed in this work that the volume of a sphere is two-thirds the volume of a cylinder surrounding it, as long as the cylinder's height and width are equal to the sphere's diameter. So proud was he of this latter discovery that he requested its illustration be engraved on his tombstone, a wish that was eventually fulfilled.

On the subject of arithmetic Archimedes wrote several essays, of which only *The Sand Reckoner*remains. Archimedes was famous for another complicated arithmetic puzzle called the Cattle Problem, in which one had to determine the number of bulls and cows of various colors, given that each cattle color was represented in a particular ratio to the others. There are an infinite number of possible solutions to the problem, but deriving them was especially challenging to the ancient Greeks, who had no knowledge of algebra.

According to the ancient historians, Archimedes was frequently called upon by King Hieron to solve practical problems. Perhaps the most famous of these was the task of determining whether King Hieron's crown was made of pure gold. Hieron believed his jeweler had stolen a portion of the gold intended for the crown, substituting an equal weight of another metal. Legend has it that Archimedes stepped into a bath and, noticing the displacement of water, conceived of a vertical buoyancyforce.

Realizing that this concept would allow him to measure the density of the king's crown in comparison to pure gold, he supposedly jumped from the tub and ran naked through the streets yelling "eureka, eureka!" ("I have found it! I have found it!"). Archimedes not only proved the crown was tainted, but went on to describe the idea of specific gravity and develop a generalized concept of buoyancy known today as Archimedes' Principle.

Archimedes recognized the mechanical advantage that could be gained by using levers, and it is said he boasted that with a long enough lever he could move the Earth. He determined the inverse mathematical relationship between the effort required to raise a load with a lever and the distance of the load from the lever's pivot point or fulcrum.

The story is told that King Hieron, skeptical of the power of mechanical advantage, challenged Archimedes to move a three-mast ship, laden with passengers and freight, that lay aground near Syracuse Harbor.

To meet the challenge Archimedes is said to have designed a system of compound pulleys. With a relatively effortless pull of a rope he was able to guide the vessel into the water. Archimedes was also interested in astronomy and made several accomplishments in this field. He built a device to estimate the size of the sun and constructed a model planetarium to demonstrate the motion of the planets.

ARYABHATA

Aryabhata is also known as Aryabhata I to distinguish him from the later mathematician of the same name who lived about 400 years later. Al-Biruni has not helped in understanding Aryabhata's life, for he seemed to believe that there were two different mathematicians called Aryabhata living at the same time. He therefore created a confusion of two different Aryabhatas which was not clarified until 1926 when B Datta showed that al-Biruni's two Aryabhatas were one and the same person.

We know the year of Aryabhata's birth since he tells us that he was twenty-three years of age when he wrote *Aryabhatiya* which he finished in 499. We have given Kusumapura, thought to be close to Pataliputra (which was refounded as Patna in Bihar in 1541), as the place of Aryabhata's birth but this is far from certain, as is even the location of Kusumapura itself.

We do know that Aryabhata wrote *Aryabhatiya* in Kusumapura at the time when Pataliputra was the capital of the Gupta empire and a major centre of learning, but there have been numerous other places proposed by historians as his birthplace. Some conjecture that he was born in south India, perhaps Kerala, Tamil Nadu or Andhra Pradesh, while others conjecture that he was born in the north-east of India, perhaps in Bengal. In it is claimed that Aryabhata was born in the Asmaka region of the Vakataka dynasty in South India although the author accepted that he lived most of his life in Kusumapura in the Gupta empire of the north. However, giving Asmaka as Aryabhata's birthplace rests on a comment made by Nilakantha Somayaji in the late 15th century. It is now thought by most historians that Nilakantha confused Aryabhata with Bhaskara I who was a later commentator on the *Aryabhatiya.*

We should note that Kusumapura became one of the two major mathematical centres of India, the other being Ujjain. Both are in the north but Kusumapura (assuming it to be close to Pataliputra) is on the Ganges and is the more northerly. Pataliputra, being the capital of the Gupta empire at the time of Aryabhata, was the centre of a communications network which allowed learning from other parts of the world to reach it easily, and also allowed the mathematical and astronomical advances made by Aryabhata and his school to reach across India and also eventually into the Islamic world.

As to the texts written by Aryabhata only one has survived. However Jha claims in that:-

... *Aryabhata was an author of at least three astronomical texts and wrote some free stanzas as well.*

The surviving text is Aryabhata's masterpiece the *Aryabhatiya* which is a small astronomical treatise written in 118 verses giving a summary of Hindu mathematics up to that time. Its mathematical section contains 33 verses giving 66 mathematical rules without proof. The *Aryabhatiya* contains an introduction of 10 verses, followed by a section on mathematics with, as we just mentioned, 33 verses, then a section of 25 verses on the reckoning of time and planetary models, with the final section of 50 verses being on the sphere and eclipses.

There is a difficulty with this layout which is discussed in detail by van der Waerden in. Van der Waerden suggests that in fact the 10 verse *Introduction* was written later than the other three sections. One reason for believing that the two parts were not intended as a whole is that the first section has a different meter to the remaining three sections. However, the problems do not stop there. We said that the first section had ten verses and indeed Aryabhata titles the section *Set of ten giti stanzas*. But it in fact contains eleven giti stanzas and two arya stanzas. Van der Waerden suggests that three verses have been added and he identifies a small number of verses in the remaining sections which he argues have also been added by a member of Aryabhata's school at Kusumapura.

The mathematical part of the *Aryabhatiya* covers arithmetic, algebra, plane trigonometry and spherical trigonometry. It also contains continued fractions, quadratic equations, sums of power series and a table of sines. Let us examine some of these in a little more detail. First we look at the system for representing numbers which Aryabhata invented and used in the *Aryabhatiya*. It consists of giving numerical values to the 33 consonants of the Indian alphabet to represent 1, 2, 3, ... , 25, 30, 40, 50, 60, 70, 80, 90, 100. The higher numbers are denoted by these consonants followed by a vowel to obtain 100, 10000, ... In fact the system allows numbers up to $10^{18}$to be represented with an alphabetical notation. Ifrah in argues that Aryabhata was also familiar with numeral symbols and the place-value system. He writes:-

... it is extremely likely that Aryabhata knew the sign for zero and the numerals of the place value system. This supposition is based on the following two facts: first, the invention of his alphabetical counting system would have been impossible without zero or the place-value system; secondly, he carries out calculations on square and cubic roots which are impossible if the numbers in question are not written according to the place-value system and zero.

Next we look briefly at some algebra contained in the *Aryabhatiya*. This work is the first we are aware of which examines integer solutions to equations of the form $by = ax + c$ and $by = ax - c$, where a, b, c are integers. The problem arose from studying the problem in astronomy of determining the periods of the planets. Aryabhata uses the kuttaka method to solve problems of this type. The word *kuttaka* means "to pulverise" and the method consisted of breaking the problem down into new problems where the coefficients became smaller and smaller with each step. The method here is essentially the use of the Euclidean algorithm to find the highest common factor of *a* and *b* but is also related to continued fractions.

Aryabhata gave an accurate approximation for p. He wrote in the *Aryabhatiya* the following:-

Add four to one hundred, multiply by eight and then add sixty-two thousand. the result is approximately the circumference of a circle of diameter twenty thousand. By this rule the relation of the circumference to diameter is given.

This gives p = $^{62832}/_{20000}$ = 3.1416 which is a surprisingly accurate value. In fact p = 3.14159265 correct to 8 places. If obtaining a value this accurate is surprising, it is perhaps even more surprising that Aryabhata does not use his accurate value for p but prefers to use v10 = 3.1622 in practice. Aryabhata does not explain how he found this accurate value but, for example, Ahmad considers this value as an approximation to half the perimeter of a regular polygon of 256 sides inscribed in the unit circle. However, in Bruins shows that this result cannot be obtained from the doubling of the number of sides. Another interesting paper discussing this accurate value of p by Aryabhata is where Jha writes:-

Aryabhata I's value of p is a very close approximation to the modern value and the most accurate among those of the ancients. There are reasons to believe that Aryabhata devised a particular method for finding this value. It is shown with sufficient grounds that Aryabhata himself used it, and several later Indian mathematicians and even the Arabs adopted it. The conjecture that Aryabhata's value of p is of Greek origin is critically examined and is found to be without foundation. Aryabhata discovered this value independently and also realised that p is an irrational number. He had the Indian background, no doubt, but excelled all his predecessors in evaluating p. Thus the credit of discovering this exact value of p may be ascribed to the celebrated mathematician, AryabhataI.

Other rules given by Aryabhata include that for summing the first *n* integers, the squares of these integers and also their cubes. Aryabhata gives formulae for the areas of a triangle and of a circle which are correct, but the formulae for the volumes of a sphere and of a pyramid are claimed to be wrong by most historians. For example Ganitanand in describes as "mathematical lapses" the fact that Aryabhata gives the incorrect formula $V = Ah/2$ for the volume of a pyramid with height h and triangular base of area A. He also appears to give an incorrect expression for the volume of a sphere. However, as is often the case, nothing is as straightforward as it appears and Elfering argues that this is not an error but rather the result of an incorrect translation. This relates to verses 6, 7, and 10 of the second section of the *Aryabhatiya* and in Elfering produces a translation which yields the correct answer for both the volume of a pyramid and for a sphere. However, in his translation Elfering translates two technical terms in a different way to the meaning which they usually have.

Without some supporting evidence that these technical terms have been used with these different meanings in other places it would still appear that Aryabhata did indeed give the incorrect formulae for these volumes.

We have looked at the mathematics contained in the *Aryabhatiya* but this is an astronomy text so we should say a little regarding the astronomy which it contains. Aryabhata gives a systematic treatment of the position of the planets in space. He gave the circumference of the earth as 4 967 yojanas and its diameter as 1 $581^1/_{24}$ yojanas. Since 1 yojana = 5 miles this gives the circumference as 24 835 miles, which is an excellent approximation to the currently accepted value of 24 902 miles. He believed that the apparent rotation of the heavens was due to the axial rotation of the Earth. This is a quite remarkable view of the nature of the solar system which later commentators could not bring themselves to follow and most changed the text to save Aryabhata from what they thought were stupid errors!

Aryabhata gives the radius of the planetary orbits in terms of the radius of the Earth/Sun orbit as essentially their periods of rotation around the Sun. He believes that the Moon and planets shine by reflected sunlight, incredibly he believes that the orbits of the planets are ellipses. He correctly explains the causes of eclipses of the Sun and the Moon. The Indian belief up to that time was that eclipses were caused by a demon called Rahu. His value for the length of the year at 365 days 6 hours 12 minutes 30 seconds is an overestimate since the true value is less than 365 days 6 hours.

ARISTOTLE

Aristotle (Aristoteles) (384 BCE – March 7, 322 BCE) was a Greek scientist and philosopher. Along with Plato, he is often considered to be one of the two most influential philosophers in Western thought.

Aristotle was born at Stagira, a Greek colony on the Macedonian peninsula Chalcidice in 384 BCE. His father, Nicomachus, was court physician to King Amyntas of Macedonia. It is believed that Aristotle's ancestors held this position under various kings of Macedonia. Aristotle was probably influenced by his father's medical knowledge; when he went to Athens at the age of 18, he was likely already trained in the investigation of natural phenomena.

From the ages of 18 to 37 Aristotle remained in Athens as a pupil of Plato and distinguished himself at the Academe. The relations between Plato and Aristotle have formed the subject of various legends, many of which depict Aristotle unfavourably. No doubt there were divergences of opinion between Plato, who took his stand on sublime, idealistic principles, and Aristotle, who even at that time showed a preference for the investigation of the facts and laws of the physical world.

It is also probable that Plato suggested that Aristotle needed restraining rather than encouragement, but not that there was an open breach of friendship. In fact, Aristotle's conduct after the death of Plato, his continued association with Xenocrates and other Platonists, and his allusions in his writings to Plato's doctrines prove that while there were conflicts of opinion between Plato and Aristotle, there was no lack of cordial appreciation or mutual forbearance. Besides this, the legends that reflect Aristotle unfavourably are traceable to the Epicureans, who were known as slanderers. If such legends were circulated widely by patristic writers such as Justin Martyr and Gregory Nazianzen, the reason lies in the exaggerated esteem Aristotle was held in by the early Christian heretics, not in any well-grounded historical tradition.

After the death of Plato (347 BCE), Aristotle went with Xenocrates to the court of Hermias, ruler of Atarneus in Asia Minor, and married his niece and adopted daughter, Pythias. In 344 BCE, Hermias was murdered in a rebellion, and Aristotle went with his family to Mytilene. Then, one or two years later, he was summoned to his native Stagira by King Philip II of Macedon to become the tutor of Alexander the Great, who was then 13.

Plutarch wrote that Aristotle not only imparted to Alexander a knowledge of ethics and politics, but also of the most profound secrets of philosophy. We have positive proof that Alexander profited by contact with the philosopher, and that Aristotle made prudent and beneficial use of his influence over the young prince.

Due to this influence, Alexander provided Aristotle with ample means for the acquisition of books and the pursuit of his scientific investigation, and it is quite likely that Alexander the Great's renowned military ability can be traced, at least in part, to his relationship with Aristotle.

In about 335 BCE, Alexander departed for his Asiatic campaign, and Aristotle, who had served as an informal adviser (more or less) since Alexander ascended the Macedonian throne, returned to Athens and opened his own school of philosophy.

He may, as Aulus Gellius says, have conducted a school of rhetoric during his former residence in Athens; but now, following Plato's example, he gave regular instruction in philosophy in a gymnasium dedicated to Apollo Lyceios, from which his school has come to be known as the Lyceum. (It was also called the Peripatetic School because Aristotle preferred to discuss problems of philosophy with his pupils while walking up and down — peripateo — the shaded walks — peripatoi — around the gymnasium.)

During the thirteen years (335 BCE-322 BCE) which he spent as teacher of the Lyceum, Aristotle composed most of his writings. Imitating Plato, he wrote "Dialogues" in which his doctrines were expounded in somewhat popular language. He also composed the several treatises (which will be mentioned below) on physics, metaphysics, and so forth, in which the exposition is more didactic and the language more technical than in the "Dialogues". These writings show to what good use he put the resources Alexander had provided for him.

They show particularly how he succeeded in bringing together the works of his predecessors in Greek philosophy, and how he pursued, either personally or through others, his investigations in the realm of natural phenomena. Pliny claimed that Alexander placed under Aristotle's orders all the hunters, fishermen, and fowlers of the royal kingdom and all the overseers of the royal forests, lakes, ponds and cattle-ranges, and Aristotle's works on zoology make this statement more believeable. Aristotle was fully informed about the doctrines of his predecessors, and Strabo asserted that he was the first to accumulate a great library.

During the last years of Aristotle's life the relations between him and Alexander the Great became very strained, owing to the disgrace and punishment of Callisthenes whom Aristotle had recommended to Alexander. Nevertheless, Aristotle continued to be regarded at Athens as a friend of Alexander and a representative of Macedonia. Consequently, when Alexander's death became known in Athens, and the outbreak occurred which led to the Lamian war, Aristotle shared in the general unpopularity of the Macedonians. The charge of impiety, which had been brought against Anaxagoras and Socrates, was now, with even less reason, brought against Aristotle.

He left the city, saying (according to many ancient authorities) that he would not give the Athenians a chance to sin a third time against philosophy. He took up residence at his country house at Chalcis, in Euboea, and there he died the following year, 322 BCE.. His death was due to a disease from which he had long suffered. The story that his death was due to hemlock poisoning, as well as the legend that he threw himself into the sea "because he could not explain the tides," is without historical foundation.

Very little is known about Aristotle's personal appearance except from hostile sources. The statues and busts of Aristotle, possibly from the first years of the Peripatetic School, represent him as sharp and keen of countenance, and somewhat below the average height. His character (as revealed by his writings), his will (which is undoubtedly genuine), fragments of his letters and the allusions of his unprejudiced contemporaries, was that of a high-minded, kind-hearted man, devoted to his family and his friends, kind to his slaves, fair to his enemies and rivals, grateful towards his benefactors.

When Platonism ceased to dominate the world of Christian speculation, and the works of Aristotle began to be studied without fear and prejudice, the personality of Aristotle appeared to the Christian writers of the 13th century, as it had to the unprejudiced pagan writers of his own day, as calm, majestic, untroubled by passion, and undimmed by any great moral defects, "the master of those who know".

AMEDEO AVOGADRO

Amedeo Avogadro (August 9, 1776–July 9, 1856) was an Italian scientist known for his research on gas volume, pressure, and temperature. He formulated the gas law known as Avogadro's law, which states that all gases, at the same temperature and pressure, have the same number of molecules per volume. Today, Avogadro is considered an important early figure in atomic theory.

Lorenzo Romano Amedeo Carlo Avogadro was born into a family of distinguished Italian lawyers in 1776. Following in his family's footsteps, he studied ecclesiastical law and began to practice on his own before eventually turning his attention to the natural sciences. In 1800, Avogadro began private studies in physics and mathematics. His very first experiments were conducted with his brother on the subject of electricity.

In 1809, Avogadro started teaching the natural sciences in a liceo (high school) in Vericelli. It was in Vericelli, while experimenting with gas densities, that Avogadro noticed something surprising:

the combination of two volumes of hydrogen gas with one volume of oxygen gas produced two volumes of water vapor. Given the understanding of gas densities at the time, Avogadro had expected the reaction to produce only one volume of water vapor. That the experiment produced two lead him to surmise that oxygen particles consisted of two atoms (he actually used the word "molecule").

In his writings, Avogadro referred to three different types of "molecules:" integral molecules (most similar to what scientists call molecules today), constituent molecules (those that are part of an element), and elementary molecules (similar to what scientists now call atoms). His study of such elementary particles was highly influential in the field of atomic theory.

Avogadro was not alone in his study of gases and molecules. Two other scientists—English chemist John Dalton and French chemist Joseph Gay-Lussac—were also exploring these topics around the same time, and their work had a strong influence on him.

Dalton is best remembered for articulating the basics of atomic theory—that all matter is composed of tiny, indivisible particles called atoms. Gay-Lussac is best remembered for his eponymous gas pressure-temperature law.

Avogadro wrote a memoria (concise note) in which he described the experimental gas law that now bears his name. He sent this memoria to De Lamétherie's Journal de Physique, de Chemie et d'Histoire naturelle, and it was published in the July 14, 1811 issue. Though his discovery is now considered a foundational aspect of chemistry, it did not receive much notice in his time.

Some historians believe that Avogadro's work was overlooked because the scientist worked in relative obscurity. Although Avogadro was aware of his contemporaries' discoveries, he did not move in their social circles and he did not begin corresponding with other major scientists until late in his career.

Very few of Avogadro's papers were translated into English and German during his lifetime. Additionally, his ideas were likely neglected because they contradicted those of more famous scientists.

In 1814, Avogadro published a memoria about gas densities, and in 1820 he became the first chair of mathematical physics at the University of Turin. As a member of a government commission on weights and measures, he helped introduce the metric system to the Piedmont region of Italy.

The standardization of measurements made it easier for scientists in different regions to understand, compare, and evaluate each other's work. Avogadro also served as a member of the Royal Superior Council on Public Instruction.

Not much is known about Avogadro's private life. In 1815, he married Felicita Mazzé; the couple had six children.

Some historical accounts indicate that Avogadro sponsored and aided a group of people planning a revolution on the island of Sardinia, which was ultimately stopped by the concession of Charles Albert's modern Constitution (Statuto Albertino). Because of his alleged political actions, Avogadro was removed as a professor at the University of Turin.

However, doubts remain as to the nature of Avogadro's association with the Sardinians. In any case, increasing acceptance of both revolutionary ideas and Avogadro's work led to his reinstatement at the University of Turin in 1833.

In 1850, Avogadro retired from the University of Turin at the age of 74. He died on July 9, 1856.

Avogadro is best known today for his eponymous gas law, which states that equal volumes of gasses, at the same temperature and pressure, contain the same number of molecules.

Avogadro's hypothesis wasn't generally accepted until 1858 (two years after Avogadro's death) when the Italian chemist Stanislao Cannizzaro was able to explain why there were some organic chemical exceptions to Avogadro's hypothesis. Cannizzaro helped clarify some of Avogadro's ideas, including his view of the relationship between atoms and molecules. He also provided empirical evidence by calculating the molecular (atomic) weights of various substances.

One of the most important contributions of Avogadro's work was his resolution of the confusion surrounding atoms and molecules (although he didn't use the term "atom"). Avogadro believed that particles could be composed of molecules and that molecules could be composed of still simpler units (which we now call "atoms").

The number of molecules in a mole (one gram molecular weight) was termed Avogadro's number (sometimes called Avogadro's constant) in honor of Avogadro's theories. Avogadro's number has been experimentally determined to be 6.023x1023 molecules per gram-mole.

BENJAMIN FRANKLIN

Benjamin Franklin was a statesmen and an inventor. Benjamin Franklin was born on January 17, 1706 in Boston, Massachusetts. His accomplishments as a scientist, publisher and statesman are particularly remarkable when considered in the context of colonial North America, which lacked the cultural and commercial institutions to nourish original ideas. He dedicated himself to the improvement of everyday life for the widest number of people and, in so doing, made an indelible mark on the emerging nation.

Benjamin Franklin initially gained acclaim through his organization of the Junto (or the Leather Apron Club), a small group of young men who engaged in business and debated morality, politics, and philosophy. Through his work with the club, Ben Franklin is credited with initiating a paid city watch, volunteer fire department, subscription library (Library Company of Philadelphia), and the American Philosophical Society, which promoted scientific and intellectual dialogue and, to this day, is one of the nation's premiere scholarly associations.

Benjamin Franklin's inventions include bifocal glasses and the iron furnace stove, a small contraption with a sliding door which burns wood on a grate, thus allowing people to cook food and heat their homes at the same time. Mid-eighteenth century scientists and inventors considered electricity to be Franklin's most remarkable area of investigation and discovery. In his famous experiment using a key and a kite during a thunderstorm, Franklin (working with his son) tested his hypothesis that lightning bolts are actually powerful electrical currents.

This work led to the invention of the lightning rod which had the dramatic effect of preventing structures from igniting and burning as the result of being struck by lightning. Although Benjamin Franklin had little formal education, he was an avid reader and writer. At twelve he was apprenticed to his brother James, a printer, who published a weekly magazine called The Spectator.

At seventeen Franklin moved to Philadelphia and quickly opened his own print shop and started publishing. Benjamin Franklin's publications reflected his democratic spirit and so were popular in format and content. Poor Richard's Almanac consisted of stories about a fictional "Poor Richard" whose trials and tribulations provided an ideal context in which Franklin could advise readers on politics, philosophy, and how to get ahead in the world.

Franklin's Pennsylvania Gazette provided information about politics to the people. Ben Franklin used political cartoons to illustrate news stories and to heighten reader appeal. The May 9, 1754 issue included Join, or Die, which is widely considered the first American political cartoon. Devised by Franklin, the cartoon reflected concern about increasing French pressure along the western frontier of the colonies.

To protest the Stamp Act provisions, which required newspapers be printed on imported, stamped paper, Franklin had the November 7, 1765 edition of the Pennsylvania Gazette printed without date, number, masthead, or imprint. In doing so, he highlighted the impact of royal policies on colonial freedom and exerted colonists' autonomy.

Recognizing the tyranny and corruption of rule by few, Benjamin Franklin and his contemporaries George Washington and Thomas Jefferson rejected the European model of aristocratic rule and crafted a system based on representational democracy.

Franklin was a member of the Continental Congress which crafted the Articles of Confederation and he helped draft the Declaration of Independence and the Constitution. These documents elevated the importance of the individual in the political process, promising the state's protection of citizens' natural, inalienable rights.

Ben Franklin also played a vital diplomatic role during the American Revolution and the early national period. In 1776, the Continental Congress sent Franklin and several others to secure a formal alliance with France, which deeply resented the loss of territory to the British during the French and Indian War. American victory over the British in the Battle of Saratoga convinced the French that the Americans were committed to independence and would be worthy partners in a formal alliance.

During the war, France contributed an estimated twelve thousand soldiers and thirty-two thousand sailors to the American war effort. In the last decade of his life, Benjamin Franklin served as a member of the Constitutional Convention and was elected president of the Pennsylvania Society for Promoting the Abolition of Slavery.

Historians have called him the quintessential American because of his creative pragmatism, scientific innovation, and democratic spirit. Inventions : Swim fins, bifocals, a glass armonica, watertight bulkheads for ships, the lightning rod, an odometer, and the wood stove (called the Franklin stove).

CHARLES BABBAGE

Charles Babbage was born on December 26, 1791 in Teignmouth, Devonshire UK, Died 1871, London; Known to some as the "Father of Computing" for his contributions to the basic design of the computer through his Analytical machine. His previous Difference Engine was a special purpose device intended for the production of tables.

While he did produce prototypes of portions of the Difference Engine, it was left to Georg and Edvard Schuetz to construct the first working devices to the same design which were successful in limited applications.

Significant Events in His Life: 1791: Born; 1810: Entered Trinity College, Cambridge; 1814: graduated Peterhouse; 1817 received MA from Cambridge; 1820: founded the Analytical Society with Herschel and Peacock; 1823: started work on the Difference Engine through funding from the British Government; 1827: published a table of logarithms from 1 to 108000; 1828: appointed to the Lucasian Chair of Mathematics at Cambridge (never presented a lecture); 1831: founded the British Association for the Advancement of Science; 1832: published "Economy of Manufactures and Machinery"; 1833: began work on the Analytical Engine; 1834: founded the Statistical Society of London; 1864: published Passages from the Life of a Philosopher; 1871: Died.

Other inventions:The cowcatcher, dynamometer, standard railroad gauge, uniform postal rates, occulting lights for lighthouses, Greenwich time signals, heliograph opthalmoscope. He also had an interest in cyphers and lock-picking, but abhorred street musicians.

BABBAGE OBSERVED : Near the northern pole of the moon there is a crater named for Charles Babbage. When he died in 1871, however, few people knew who he was. Only one carriage (the Duchess of Somerset's) followed in the burial procession that took his remains to Kensal Green Cemetery. The Royal Society printed no obituary, and the Times ridiculed him. The parts of the Difference Engine that had seemed possible of completion in 1830 gathered dust in the Museum of King's College.

In 1878 The Cayley committee told the government not to bother constructing Babbage's Analytical Engine. By the 1880's Babbage was known primarily for his reform of mathematics at Cambridge. In 1899 the magazine Temple Bar reported that "the present generation appears to have forgotten Babbage and his calculating machine".

In 1908, after being preserved for 37 years in alcohol, Babbage's brain was dissected by Sir Victor Horsley of the Royal Society. Horsley had to remind the society that Babbage had been a "very profound thinker".

Charles Babbage was born in Devonshire in 1791. Like John von Neumann, he was the son of a banker - Benjamin (Old Five Percent) Babbage. He attended Trinity Collcgc, Cambridgc, receiving his MA in 1817. As the inventor of the first universal digital computer, he can indeed be considered a profound thinker.

The use of Jacquard punch cards, of chains and subassemblies, and ultimately the logical structure of the modern computer - all come from Babbage.

Popularly, Babbage is a sort of Abner Doubleday of data processing, a colorful fellow whose portrait hangs in the anteroom but whose actual import is slight. He is thought about, if at all, as a funny sort of distracted character with dirty collar. But Babbage was much more than that. He was an amazing intelligence.

Babbage was an aesthete, but not a typical Victorian one. He found beauty in things: in stamped buttons, stomach pumps, railways and tunnels, in man's mastery over nature.

A social man, he was obliged to attend the theater. While others dozed at Mozart, Babbage grew restless. "Somewhat fatigued with the opera [Don Juan]", he writes in the autobiographical Passages From the Life of a Philosopher, "I went behind the scenes to look at the mechanism".

There, a workman offered to show him around. Deserted when his Cicerone answered a cue, he met two actors dressed at "devils with long forked tails". The devils were to convey Juan, via trapdoor and stage elevator, to hell.

In his box at the German Opera some time later (again not watching the stage), Babbage noticed "in the cloister scene at midnight" that his companion's white bonnet had a pink tint. He thought about "producing colored lights for theatrical representation". In order to have something on which to shine his experimental lights, Babbage devised "Alethes and Iris", a ballet in which 60 damsels in white were to dance.

In the final scene, a series of dioramas were to represent Alethes' travels. One diorama would show animals "whose remains are contained in each successive layer of the earth. In the lower portions, symptoms of increasing heat show themselves until the centre is reached, which contains a liquid transparent sea, consisting of some fluid at white heat, which, however, is filled up with little infinitesimal eels, all of one sort, wriggling eternally".

Two fire engines stood ready for the "experiment of the dance", as Babbage termed the rehearsal. Dancers "danced and attitudinized" while he shone colored lights on them. But the theater manager feared fire, and the ballet was never publicly staged.

Babbage enjoyed fire. He once was baked in an oven at 265oF for "five or six minutes without any great discomfort", and on another occasion was lowered into Mt. Vesuvius to view molten lava. Did he ponder Hell? He had considered becoming a cleric, but this was not an unusual choice for the affluent graduate with little interest in business or law.

In 1837 he published his Ninth Bridgewater Treatise, to reconcile his scientific beliefs with Christian dogma. Babbage argued that miracles were not, as Hume write, violations of laws of nature, but could exist in a mechanistic world. As Babbage could program long series on his calculating machines, God could program similar irregularities in nature.

Babbage investigated biblical miracles. "In the course of his analysis", wrote B. V. Bowden in Faster than Thought (Pitman, London, 1971), "he made the assumption that the chance of a man rising from the dead is one in 10^12". Miracles are not, as he wrote in Passages From the Life of a Philosopher, "the breach of established laws, but... indicate the existence of far higher laws".

CHARLES DARWIN

The English naturalist Charles Robert Darwin (1809-1882) discovered that natural selection was the agent for the transmutation of organisms during evolution, as did Alfred Russel Wallace independently. Darwin presented his theory in "Origin of Species."

The concept of evolution by descent dates at least from classical Greek philosophers. In the 18th century Carl Linnaeus postulated limited mutability of species by descent and hybridization. Charles Darwin's grandfather, Erasmus Darwin, and the Chevalier de Lamarck were the chief proponents of evolution about 1800. Such advocacy had little impact on the majority of naturalists, concerned to identify species, the stability of which was considered essential for their work.

Natural theology regarded the perfection of adaptation between structure and mode of life in organisms as evidence for a beneficent, all-seeing, all-planning Creator. Organic structure, planned in advance for a preordained niche, was unchanged from the moment of creation. Variations in structure in these earthly imperfect versions of the Creator's idea were minor and impermanent.

In 1815 William Smith had demonstrated a sequence of fossil populations in time. Charles Lyell, adopting James Hutton's uniformitarian view that present conditions and processes were clues to the past history of the earth, wrote his Principles of Geology (1830-1833), which Darwin on his *Beagle* circumnavigation found most apt for his own geological observations.

Fossils in South America and apparent anomalies of animal distribution triggered the task for Darwin of assembling a vast range of material. A reading of Thomas Malthus's *Essay on the Principle of Population* in 1838 completed Darwin's conceptual scheme.

Critics, for whom the *Origin* is paramount among Darwin's considerable output, have accused him of vacillation and procrastination. But recent study of unpublished manuscripts and his entire works reveal a continuity of purpose and integrity of effort to establish the high probability of the genetic relationship through descent in all forms of life. Man is dethroned as the summit of creation and as the especial concern of the Creator. This revolution in thought has had an effect on every kind of human activity.

Darwin was born on February 12, 1809, at Shrewsbury, the fifth child of Robert and Susannah Darwin. His mother, who was the daughter of the famous potter Josiah Wedgwood, died when Charles was 8, and he was reared by his sisters.

In 1825 Darwin went to Edinburgh University to study medicine. He found anatomy and *materia medica* dull and surgery unendurable. In 1828 he entered Christ's College, Cambridge, with the idea of taking Anglican orders. He attended John Stevens Henslow's course in botany, started a collection of beetles that became famous, and read widely. William Paley's *Natural Theology*

(1802) delighted Darwin by its clear logical presentation, and he later regarded this study as the most worthwhile benefit from Cambridge. He received his bachelor's degree in 1831.

On Henslow's recommendation Darwin was offered the position of naturalist for the second voyage of H. M. S. *Beagle* to survey the coast of Patagonia and Tierra del Fuego and complete observations of longitude by circumnavigation with a formidable array of chronometers. The *Beagle* left on Dec. 27, 1831, and returned on Oct. 2, 1836. During the voyage Darwin spent 535 days at sea and roughly 1200 on land.

Darwin kept his field observations in notebooks with the specimens listed serially and their place and time of collection documented. On July 24, 1834, he wrote: "My notes are becoming bulky. I have about 600 small quarto pages full; about half of this is Geology the other imperfect descriptions of animals; with the latter I make it a rule to describe those parts which cannot be seen in specimens in spirits.

I keep my private Journal distinct from the above." Toward the end of the voyage, when sea passages were long, he copied his notes and arranged them to accord with systematics, concentrating on range and habits. Geology was prepared with fewer inhibitions; he wrote from Mauritius in April 1836: "It is a rare piece of good fortune for me that of the many errant (in ships) Naturalists there have been few, or rather no, Geologists. I shall enter the field unopposed."

During the trip Darwin discovered the relevance of Lyell's uniformitarian views to the structure of St. Jago (Cape Verde Islands). He found that small locally living forms closely resembled large terrestrial fossil mammals embedded between marine shell layers and that the local sea was populated with living occupants of similar shells. He also observed the overlapping distribution on the continuous Patagonian plain of two closely related but distinct species of ostrich.

CHRISTIAAN HUYGENS

Christiaan Huygens came from an important Dutch family. His father Constantin Huygens had studied natural philosophy and was a diplomat. It was through him that Christiaan was to gain access to the top scientific circles of the times. In particular Constantin had many contacts in England and corresponded regularly with Mersenne and was a friend of Descartes.

Tutored at home by private teachers until he was 16 years old, Christiaan learned geometry, how to make mechanical models and social skills such as playing the lute. His mathematical education was clearly influenced by Descartes who was an occasional visitor at the Huygens' home and took a great interest in the mathematical progress of the young Christiaan.

Christiaan Huygens studied law and mathematics at the University of Leiden from 1645 until 1647. Van Schooten tutored him in mathematics while he was in Leiden. From 1647 until 1649 he continued to study law and mathematics but now at the College of Orange at Breda. Here he was fortunate to have another skilled teacher of mathematics, John Pell. Through his father's contact with Mersenne, a correspondence between Huygens and Mersenne began around this time. Mersenne challenged Huygens to solve a number of problems including the shape of the rope supported from its ends. Although he failed at this problem he did solve the related problem of how to hang weights on the rope so that it hung in a parabolic shape.

In 1649 Huygens went to Denmark as part of a diplomatic team and hoped to continue to Stockholm to visit Descartes but the weather did not allow him to make this journey. He followed the visit to Denmark with others around Europe including Rome.

Huygens's first publications in 1651 and 1654 considered mathematical problems. The 1651 publication *Cyclometriae* showed the fallacy in methods proposed by Gregory of Saint-Vincent, who had claimed to have squared the circle. Huygens' 1654 work *De Circuli Magnitudine Inventa* was a more major work on similar topics.

Huygens soon turned his attention to lens grinding and telescope construction. Around 1654 he devised a new and better way of grinding and polishing lenses. Using one of his own lenses, Huygens detected, in 1655, the first moon of Saturn. In this same year he made his first visit to Paris. He informed the mathematicians in Paris including Boulliau of his discovery and in turn Huygens learnt of the work on probability carried out in a correspondence between Pascal and Fermat. On his return to Holland Huygens wrote a small work *De Ratiociniis in Ludo Aleae* on the calculus of probabilities, the first printed work on the subject.

The following year he discovered the true shape of the rings of Saturn. However others had different theories including Roberval and Boulliau. Boulliau had failed to detect Saturn's moon Titan so Huygens realised that he was using an inferior telescope. By 1656 Huygens was able to confirm his ring theory to Boulliau and the results were reported to the Paris group. In *Systema*

Saturnium (1659), Huygens explained the phases and changes in the shape of the ring. Some, including the Jesuit Fabri, attacked not only Huygens theories but also his observations. However by 1665 even Fabri was persuaded to accept Huygens' ring theory as improving telescopes confirmed his observations.

Work in astronomy required accurate timekeeping and this prompted Huygens to tackle this problem. In 1656 he patented the first pendulum clock, which greatly increased the accuracy of time measurement. His work on the pendulum was related to other mathematical work which he had been doing on the cycloid as a result of the challenge by Pascal. Huygens believed that a pendulum swinging in a large are would be more useful at sea and he invented the cycloidal pendulum with this in mind. He built several pendulum clocks to determine longitude at sea and they underwent sea trials in 1662 and again in 1686. In the *Horologium Oscillatorium sive de motu pendulorum* (1673) he described the theory of pendulum motion. He also derived the law of centrifugal force for uniform circular motion. As a result of this Huygens, Hooke, Halley and Wren formulated the inverse-square law of gravitational attraction.

Huygens returned to Paris in 1660 and went to meetings of various scientific societies there. He wrote, in a letter to his brother:-

... there is a meeting every Tuesday [at Montmor's house] where twenty or thirty illustrious men are found together. I never fail to go ... I have also been occasionally to the house of M Rohault, who expounds the philosophy of M Descartes and does very fine experiments with good reasoning on them.

At these societies he met many mathematicians including Roberval, Carcavi, Pascal, Pierre Petit, Desargues and Sorbière. After Pascal visited him in December 1660 Huygens wrote

... we talked of the force of water rarefied in cannons and of flying, I showed him my telescopes...

In 1661 Huygens visited London, particularly to find out more about the newly forming Royal Society meeting at that time in Gresham College. He was greatly impressed with Wallis and the other English scientists whom he met and, from this time on, he was to continue his contacts with this group. He showed his telescopes to the English scientists and they proved superior to those in use in England. The Duke and Duchess of York came to observe the Moon and Saturn through Huygens' telescope. While in London Huygens saw Boyle's vacuum pump and he was impressed. After his return to the Hague he carried out a number of Boyle's experiments for himself. Huygens was elected to the Royal Society of London in 1663.

At this time Huygens patented his design of pendulum clock with the solution of the longitude problem in mind. In 1665 he learnt that the Royal Society was investigating other forms of clock, in particular Hooke was experimenting with a spring regulated clock. Huygens wrote to Hooke doubting this approach which he felt would be unduly affected by temperature changes. Despite this Huygens did begin to experiment with clocks regulated by springs, but their accuracy was poorer than his pendulum clocks.

Huygens accepted an invitation from Colbert in 1666 to become part of the Académie Royale des Sciences. He arrived in Paris that year to discover that the Society was not yet organised. After meetings were held with Roberval, Carcavi, Auzout, Frenicle de Bessy, Auzout and Buot in Colbert's library the Society moved to the Bibliothèque du Roi where Huygens took up residence. He assumed leadership of the group basing much on his knowledge of the way the Royal Society operated in England.

Huygens' work on the collision of elastic bodies showed the error Descartes' laws of impact and his memoir on the topic was sent to the Royal Society in 1668. The Royal Society had posed a question on impact and Huygens proved by experiment that the momentum in a fixed direction before the collision of two bodies is equal to the momentum in that direction after the collision. Wallis and Wren also answered this question.

Circular motion was a topic which Huygens took up at this time but he also continued to think about Descartes' theory of gravity based on vortices. He seems to have shown signs of being unhappy with Descartes' theory around this time but he still addressed the

Académie on this topic in 1669 although after his address Roberval and Mariotte argued strongly, and correctly, against Descartes' theory and this may have influenced Huygens.

From his youth Huygens' health had never been robust and in 1670 he had a serious illness which resulted in him leaving Paris for Holland. Before he left Paris, believing himself to be close to death he asked that his unpublished papers on mechanics be sent to the Royal Society. The secretary to the English ambassador was called and described Huygens' reasons:-

... he fell into a discourse concerning the Royal Society in England which he said was an assembly of the choicest wits in Christendom ... he said he chose to deposit those little labours ... in their hands sooner than any else. ... he said he did foresee the dissolution of this Academy because it was mixed with tinctures of envy because it was supported upon suppositions of profit because it wholly depended upon the humour of a prince and the favour of a minister...

By 1671 Huygens returned to Paris. However in 1672 Louis XIV invaded the Low Countries and Huygens found himself in the extremely difficult position of being in an important position in Paris at a time France was at war with his own country. Scientists of this era felt themselves above political wars and Huygens was able, with much support from his friends, to continue his work.

In 1672 Huygens and Leibniz met in Paris and thereafter Leibniz was a frequent visitor to the Académie. In fact Leibniz owes much to Huygens from whom he learnt much of his mathematics. In this same year Huygens learnt of Newton's work on the telescope and on light. He, quite wrongly, criticised Newton's theory of light, in particular his theory of colour. His own work, *Horologium Oscillatorium sive de motu pendulorum* appeared in 1673 and showed that Huygens had moved far from Descartes' influence.

Horologium Oscillatorium contains work on the pendulum. In it Huygens proves that the cycloid is tautochronous, an important theoretical result but one which had little practical application to the pendulum. He also solves the problem of the compound pendulum. However there is much more than work on pendulums. Huygens describes the descent of bodies in a vacuum, either vertically or along curves. He defines evolutes and involutes of curves and, after giving some elementary properties, finds the evolutes of the cycloid and of the parabola. Huygens attempts for the first time in this work to study the dynamics of bodies rather than particles.

Papin worked as an assistant to Huygens around this time and after he left to work with Boyle, Huygens was joined by Tschirnhaus. Another bout of illness in 1676 saw Huygens return to the Hague again. He spent two years there, in particular studying the double refraction Bartholin had discovered in Iceland spar crystal. He also worked on the velocity of light which he believed was finite and was pleased to hear of Römer's experiments which gave an approximate velocity for light determined by observing Jupiter's moons.

By 1678 Huygens had returned to Paris. In that year his *Traité de la lumiere* appeared, in it Huygens argued in favour of a wave theory of light. Huygens stated that an expanding sphere of light behaves as if each point on the wave front were a new source of radiation of the same frequency and phase. However his health became even more unreliable and he became ill in 1679 and then again in 1681 when he returned to the Hague for the last time. La Hire, who had always argued against foreigners in the Académie, sent his best wishes to Huygens but he clearly hoped that he would not return so that he might himself might acquire his position.

The longitude problem had remained a constant cause for Huygens to continue work on clocks all his life. Again after his health returned he worked on a new marine clock during 1682 and, with the Dutch East India Company showing interest, he worked hard on the clocks.

Colbert died in 1683 and a return to Paris without the support of his patron seemed impossible. His father died in 1687, having reached 91 years of age, and the following year his brother left for England. Huygens missed having people around him with whom he could discuss scientific topics. In 1689 he came to England.

In England Huygens met Newton, Boyle and others in the Royal Society. It is not known what discussions went on between Huygens and Newton but we do know that Huygens had a great admiration for Newton but at the same time did not believe the theory of universal gravitation which he said *appears to me absurd.*

In some sense of course Huygens was right, how can one believe that two distant masses attract one another when there is nothing between them, nothing in Newton's theory explains how one mass can possible even know the other mass is there. Writing about Newton and the *Principia* some time later Huygens wrote:-

I esteem his understanding and subtlety highly, but I consider that they have been put to ill use in the greater part of this work, where the author studies things of little use or when he builds on the improbable principle of attraction.

He departed with much sadness at the thoughts of his scientific isolation in Holland.

In the final years of his life Huygens composed one of the earliest discussions of extraterrestrial life, published after his death as the *Cosmotheoros* (1698). He continued to work on improving lenses and on a spring regulated clock and on new pendulum clocks.

DANIEL BERNOULLI

Daniel Bernoulli was born on 8 Feb 1700 in Groningen, Netherlands. He was the son of Johann Bernoulli. He was born in Groningen while his father held the chair of mathematics there. His older brother was Nicolaus(II) Bernoulli and his uncle was Jacob Bernoulli so he was born into a family of leading mathematicians but also into a family where there was unfortunate rivalry, jealousy and bitterness.

When Daniel was five years old the family returned to their native city of Basel where Daniel's father filled the chair of mathematics left vacant on the death of his uncle Jacob Bernoulli. When Daniel was five years old his younger brother Johann(II) Bernoulli was born. All three sons would go on to study mathematics but this was not the course that Johann Bernoulli planned for Daniel.

Johann Bernoulli's father had tried to force Johann into a business career and he had resisted strongly. Rather strangely Johann Bernoulli now tried exactly the same with his own son Daniel.

First however Daniel was sent to Basel University at the age of 13 to study philosophy and logic.

He obtained his baccalaureate examinations in 1715 and went on to obtain his master's degree in 1716. Daniel, like his father, really wanted to study mathematics and during the time he studied philosophy at Basel, he was learning the methods of the calculus from his father and his older brother Nicolaus(II) Bernoulli.

Johann was determined that Daniel should become a merchant and he tried to place him in an apprenticeship. However Daniel was as strongly opposed to this as his own father had been and soon Johann relented but certainly not as far as to let Daniel study mathematics. Johann declared that there was no money in mathematics and so he sent Daniel back to Basel University to study medicine. This Daniel did spending time studying medicine at Heidelberg in 1718 and Strasbourg in 1719. He returned to Basel in 1720 to complete his doctorate in medicine.

By this stage Johann Bernoulli was prepared to teach his son more mathematics while he studied medicine and Daniel studied his father's theories of kinetic energy. What he learned on the conservation of energy from his father he applied to his medical studies and Daniel wrote his doctoral dissertation on the mechanics of breathing. So like his father Daniel had applied mathematical physics to medicine in order to obtain his medical doctorate.

Daniel wanted to embark on an academic career like his father so he applied for two chairs at Basel. His application for the chair of anatomy and botany was decided by drawing of lots and he was unlucky in this game of chance.

The next chair to fall vacant at Basel that Daniel applied for was the chair of logic, but again the game of chance of the final selection by drawing of lots went against him. Having failed to obtain an academic post, Daniel went to Venice to study practical medicine.

In Venice Daniel was severely ill and so was unable to carry out his intention of travelling to Padua to further his medical studies.

However, while in Venice he worked on mathematics and his first mathematical work was published in 1724 when, with Goldbach's assistance, *Mathematical exercises* was published. This consisted of four separate parts being four topics that had attracted his interest while in Venice.

The first part described the game of faro and is of little importance other than showing that Daniel was learning about probability at this time. The second part was on the flow of water from a hole in a container and discussed Newton's theories (which were incorrect).

Daniel had not solved the problem of pressure by this time but again the work shows that his interest was moving in this direction. His medical work on the flow of blood and blood pressure also gave him an interest in fluid flow. The third part of *Mathematical exercises* was on the Riccati differential equation while the final part was on a geometry question concerning figures bounded by two arcs of a circle.

While in Venice, Daniel had also designed an hour glass to be used at sea so that the trickle of sand was constant even when the ship was rolling in heavy seas. He submitted his work on this to the Paris Academy and in 1725, the year he returned from Italy to Basel, he learnt that he had won the prize of the Paris Academy. Daniel had also attained fame through his work *Mathematical exercises* and on the strength of this he was invited to take up the chair of mathematics at St Petersburg.

His brother Nicolaus(II) Bernoulli was also offered a chair of mathematics at St Petersburg so in late 1725 the two brothers travelled to St Petersburg. Within eight months of their taking up the appointments in St Petersburg Daniel's brother died of fever. Daniel was left, greatly saddened at the loss of his brother and also very unhappy with the harsh climate.

He thought of returning to Basel and wrote to his father telling him how unhappy he was in St Petersburg. Johann Bernoulli was able to arrange for one of his best pupils, Leonard Euler, to go to St Petersburg to work with Daniel. Euler arrived in 1727 and this period in St Petersburg, which Daniel left in 1733, was to be his most productive time.

One of the topics which Daniel studied in St Petersburg was that of vibrating systems. As Straub writes in [1]:-

From 1728, *Bernoulli and Euler dominated the mechanics of flexible and elastic bodies, in that year deriving the equilibrium curves for these bodies. ... Bernoulli determined the shape that a perfectly flexible thread assumes when acted upon by forces of which one component is vertical to the curve and the other is parallel to a given direction. Thus, in one stroke he derived the entire series of such curves as the velaria, lintearia, catenaria...*

While in St Petersburg he made one of his most famous discoveries when he defined the simple nodes and the frequencies of oscillation of a system. He showed that the movements of strings of musical instruments are composed of an infinite number of harmonic vibrations all superimposed on the string.

A second important work which Daniel produced while in St Petersburg was one on probability and political economy. Daniel makes the assumption that the moral value of the increase in a person's wealth is inversely proportional to the amount of that wealth. He then assigns probabilities to the various means that a person has to make money and deduces an expectation of increase in moral expectation. Daniel applied some of his deductions to insurance.

Undoubtedly the most important work which Daniel Bernoulli did while in St Petersburg was his work on hydrodynamics. Even the term itself is based on the title of the work which he produced called *Hydrodynamica* and, before he left St Petersburg, Daniel left a draft copy of the book with a printer. However the work was not published until 1738 and although he revised it considerably between 1734 and 1738, it is more the presentation that he changed rather then the substance.

This work contains for the first time the correct analysis of water flowing from a hole in a container. This was based on the principle of conservation of energy which he had studied with his father in

1720. Daniel also discussed pumps and other machines to raise water.

One remarkable discovery appears in Chapter 10 of *Hydrodynamica* where Daniel discussed the basis for the kinetic theory of gases. He was able to give the basic laws for the theory of gases and gave, although not in full detail, the equation of state discovered by Van der Waals a century later.

Daniel Bernoulli was not happy in St Petersburg, despite the obvious scientific advantage of working with Euler. By 1731 he was applying for posts in Basel but probability seemed to work against him and he would lose out in the ballot for the post.

The post was neither one in mathematics nor physics but Daniel preferred to return to Basel and give lectures on botany rather than remain in St Petersburg. By this time his younger brother Johann(II) Bernoulli was also with him in St Petersburg and they left St Petersburg in 1733, making visits to Danzig, Hamburg, Holland and Paris before returning to Basel in 1734.

Daniel Bernoulli submitted an entry for the Grand Prize of the Paris Academy for 1734 giving an application of his ideas to astronomy. This had unfortunate consequences since Daniel's father, Johann Bernoulli, also entered for the prize and their entries were declared joint winners of the Grand Prize. The result of this episode of the prize of the Paris Academy had unhappy consequences for Daniel. His father was furious to think that his son had been rated as his equal and this resulted in a breakdown in relationships between the two.

The outcome was that Daniel found himself back in Basel but banned from his father's house. Whether this caused Daniel to become less interested in mathematics or whether it was the fact that his academic position was a non mathematical one, certainly Daniel never regained the vigour for mathematical research that he showed in St Petersburg.

Although Daniel had left St Petersburg, he began an immediate correspondence with Euler and the two exchanged many ideas on vibrating systems. Euler used his great analytic skills to put many of Daniel's physical insights into a rigorous mathematical form.

Daniel continued to work on polishing his masterpiece *Hydrodynamica* for publication and added a chapter on the force of reaction of a jet of fluid and the force of a jet of water on an inclined plane. In this chapter, Chapter 13, he also discussed applications to the propulsion of ships.

The 1737 prize of the Paris Academy also had a nautical theme, the best shape for a ship's anchor, and Daniel Bernoulli was again the joint winner of this prize, this time jointly with Poleni. *Hydrodynamica* was published in 1738 but, in the following year Johann Bernoulli published *Hydraulica* which is largely based on his son's work but Johann tried to make it look as if Daniel had based *Hydrodynamica* on *Hydraulica* by predating the date of publication on his book to 1732 instead of its real date which is probably 1739.

This was a disgraceful attempt by Johann to gain credit for work which was not his and at the same time to discredit his own son and shows the depths to which the bad feeling between them had reached.

It is fair to say that there is no evidence that Daniel was in any way to blame for the breakdown of relationships with his father. Rather the reverse since there is evidence that he tried to mend the relationship with such acts as describing himself on the frontispiece of *Hydrodynamica* as 'Daniel Bernoulli, son of Johann'.

Another sign that Daniel was not jealous of members of his own family in the way the Johann Bernoulli and Jacob Bernoulli had been is the fact that he did produce joint work with his younger brother Johann(II) Bernoulli.

Botany lectures were not what Daniel wanted and things became better for him in 1743 when he was able to exchange these for physiology lectures. In 1750, however, he was appointed to the chair of physics and taught physics at Basel for 26 years until 1776.

He gave some remarkable physics lectures with experiments performed during the lectures. Based on experimental evidence he was able to conjecture certain laws which were not verified until many years later. Among these was Coulomb's law in electrostatics.

Daniel Bernoulli did produce other excellent scientific work during these many years back in Basel. In total he won the Grand Prize of the Paris Academy 10 times, for topics in astronomy and nautical topics.

He won in 1740 (jointly with Euler) for work on Newton's theory of the tides; in 1743 and 1746 for essays on magnetism; in 1747 for a method to determine time at sea; in 1751 for an essay on ocean currents; in 1753 for the effects of forces on ships; and in 1757 for proposals to reduce the pitching and tossing of a ship in high seas.

Another important aspect of Daniel Bernoulli's work that proved important in the development of mathematical physics was his acceptance of many of Newton's theories and his use of these together with the tolls coming from the more powerful calculus of Leibniz.

Daniel worked on mechanics and again used the principle of conservation of energy which gave an integral of Newton's basic equations. He also studied the movement of bodies in a resisting medium using Newton's methods.

He also continued to produce good work on the theory of oscillations and in a paper he gave a beautiful account of the oscillation of air in organ pipes. His strengths and weaknesses are summed up by Straub in:-

Bernoulli's active and imaginative mind dealt with the most varied scientific areas. Such wide interests, however, often prevented him from carrying some of his projects to completion.

It is especially unfortunate that he could not follow the rapid growth of mathematics that began with the introduction of partial differential equations into mathematical physics.

Nevertheless he assured himself a permanent place in the history of science through his work and discoveries in hydrodynamics, his anticipation of the kinetic theory of gases, a novel method for calculating the value of an increase in assets, and the demonstration that the most common movement of a string in a musical instrument is composed of the superposition of an infinite number of harmonic vibrations...

Daniel Bernoulli was much honoured in his own lifetime. He was elected to most of the leading scientific societies of his day including those in Bologna, St Petersburg, Berlin, Paris, London, Bern, Turin, Zurich and Mannheim. Daniel Bernoulli died on 17 March 1782 in Basel, Switzerland.

DMITRI MENDELEEV

Born in Siberia, the last of at least 14 children, Dmitri Mendeleev revolutionized our understanding of the properties of atoms and created a table that probably adorns every chemistry classroom in the world.

After his father went blind and could no longer support the family, Mendeleev's mother started a glass factory to help make ends meet. But just as Mendeleev was finishing high school, his father died and the glass factory burned down. With most of her other children now out on their own, his mother took her son to St. Petersburg, working tirelessly and successfully to get him into college.

In the late 1860's, Mendeleev began working on his great achievement: the periodic table of the elements. By arranging all of the 63 elements then known by their atomic weights, he managed to organize them into groups possessing similar properties. Where a gap existed in the table, he predicted a new element would one day be found and deduced its properties. And he was right. Three of those elements were found during his lifetime: gallium, scandium, and germanium.

The discovery of these elements provided the strongest support for his periodic table, a cornerstone both in chemistry and in our understanding of how the universe is put together (reference). In 1849, with nothing left for the family at Aremziansk, Maria loaded up the family's belongings and headed for Moscow. At this point the family included Maria, Dmitri, and Elizabeth (Dmitri's older sister).

In Moscow, they entered a climate of considerable political unrest, which made the university reluctant to admit anyone from outside of Moscow. Mendeleev was rejected. Maria did not give up, however, and the family headed for St. Petersburg.

Again, they encountered similar turmoil but this time they found a friend of Ivan's working at the Pedagogical Institute, his father's school. With a little persuasion, Dmitri was allowed to take the entrance exams, which he passed, not with honors but well enough to be admitted to the science teacher training program on a full scholarship. He entered the university in the fall of 1850. Maria died shortly after Dmitri's acceptance at St. Petersburg, followed a few short months later by Elizabeth; both died from tuberculosis. Mendeleev was left alone to face his work at the university, but was to later eulogize his mother in his book on Solutions.

"This investigation is dedicated to the memory of a mother by her youngest offspring. Conducting a factory she could educate him only by her own work. She instructed by example, corrected with love, and in order to devote him to science she left Siberia with him, spending thus her last resources and strength."

"When dying she said, '*Refrain from illusions, insist on work and not on words. Patiently search divine and scientific truth.*' She understood how often dialectical methods deceive, how much there is still to be learned, and how, with the aid of science without violence, with love but firmness, all superstition, untruth and error are removed, bringing in their stead the safety of undiscovered truth, freedom for further development, general welfare, and inward happiness. Dmitri Mendeleev regards as sacred a mother's dying words."

Dmitri fell right into his work at St. Petersburg. His studies progressed rapidly until his third year. At that point he was struck with an illness that caused him to be bedridden for the next year. He continued his studies, however, with professors and fellow students visiting him to give him assignments, etc. Mendeleev graduated on time and was awarded the medal of excellence for being first in his class.

Dmitri's illness did not improve. His doctor suggested that he had tuberculosis and that, at most, he had two years to live providing he moved to a more suitable climate. Mendeleev already had his life's ambitions in mind and, hoping to extend his life as long as possible, he moved to Simferopol in the Crimean Peninsula near the Black Sea in 1855 as chief science master of the gymnasium. He was 21 years old. At this point in his life he was driven by "the vision of the Russian people whom he knew he could aid through science." Needless to say, his move to the south was very beneficial. He progressively regained his strength to the point where the doctors found no sign of tuberculosis in his system.

In 1856, Mendeleev returned to St. Petersburg and defended his master's thesis: "*Research and Theories on Expansion of Substances due to Heat.*" Following his masters program, Dmitri focused his life on his career of teaching and research. He was essentially a teacher devoted to his work and to his students; he was next a lover of his country and of his fellow men. The first led to his books and the periodic table, while the latter gave rise to his studies of chemical technology and the organization of Russia's industries, agriculture, transport meteorology and metrology.

In 1859, he was assigned by the Minister of Public Instruction to go abroad to study and develop scientific and technological innovations. Between 1859 and 1861 he studied the densities of gases with Regnault in Paris and the workings of the spectroscope with Kirchoff in Heidelberg.

He also pursued studies of capillarity and surface tension that led to his theory of "absolute boiling point," later known as critical temperature. While in Heidelberg he made the acquaintance of A.P. Borodin, a chemist who was to achieve greater reknown as a composer.

In 1860 at the Chemical Congress at Karlsruhe, Mendeleev had the opportunity to hear Cannizzaro discuss his work on atomic weights. These people greatly influenced the work which Mendeleev would pursue the rest of his life.

Following his trip abroad, the Russian chemist returned to his homeland where he settled down to a life of teaching and research in St. Petersburg.

In 1863 he was named Professor of Chemistry at the Technological Institute and, in 1866, he became Professor of Chemistry at the University and was made Doctor of Science for his dissertation "On the Combinations of Water with Alcohol". As will be seen, his research findings were expansive and beneficial to the Russian people.

Dmitri was always in touch with the classroom. Much of his lab work, including that on the periodic chart, occurred in his spare time following his lectures. He truly enjoyed educating the people, and they, in turned enjoyed his efforts: ...*For me it was a revelation, a beautiful improvisation, a stimulant to the intellect which left deep traces on my development.*

Mendeleev not only taught in the university classrooms but anywhere he travelled. Many excerpts discuss his journeys by train where he would travel third class with the mouzhiks (peasants). It was on those journeys that he would share his findings about agriculture with the peasants over a cup of tea.

The admiration that Mendeleev had for the people of Russia was reciprocated by the people. On the trains the mouzhiks would all gather round to see and talk with the man. The university students also adored him. Crowds of students would fill lecture halls to hear him speak of chemistry.

For Mendeleev, science was always the most important subject, but in that time period of unrest, just as today, science could be expanded to the realms of politics and social inequality. Mendeleev was not afraid to express his views on these topics:

There exists everywhere a medium in things, determined by equilibrium. The Russian proverb says, '*Too much salt or too little salt is alike an evil*.' It is the same in political and social relations... It is the function of science to discover the existence of a general reign of order in nature and to find the causes governing this order. And this refers in equal measure to the relations of man, social and political, and to the entire universe as a whole.

These profound thoughts of order led him to the discovery of the periodic law, among other things, but also led to his resignation from the University on August 17, 1890. Throughout his life he witnessed a country repressed and in turmoil.

As he grew older and more famous, he used his new-found prestige and power to try to speak out against repression. The most all penetrating spirit before which will open the possibility of tilting not tables, but planets, is the spirit of free human inquiry. Believe only in that. His resignation from the university came as the result of carrying a student petition to the Minister of Education.

The Minister refused to acknowledge the requests, stating that Mendeleev should keep to teaching and not involve himself with students and politics. Mendeleev's final lecture at the University of St. Petersburg was broken up by police who feared that he might lead the students in an uprising.

Dmitri's personal life also appears to have been in turmoil for many years. In 1863, with the heavy influence of his sister Olga, Dmitri married Feozva Nikitchna Lascheva. They had two children, a boy named Volodya, and a daughter named Olga. Mendeleev never really loved Feozva and actually spent little time with her. One story suggests that, at one point in their life together, Feozva asked Mendeleev if he was married to her or to science; his response was that he was married to both unless that was bigamy, in which case he was married to science.

In January 1882, he divorced Feozva so he could marry his niece's best friend, Anna Ivanova Popova. According to the Orthodox Church, Mendeleev was officially a bigamist; however, he was so famous in Russia that the Czar said "*Mendeleev has two wives, yes, but I have only one Mendeleev*".

Anna was considerably younger than Dmitri but the two loved each other very much and were together until his death. They had four children: Liubov, Ivan, and twins Vassili and Maria. Anna also had considerable influence over Mendeleev's views on art, and he was elected to the Academy of Arts for both his insightful criticism and his painting.

As he grew older it also became apparent that personal appearance became less and less significant to him. Many stories abound relating to the idea that in his later years, Dmitri would only cut his hair and beard once a year. He would not even cut it by request of the tsar. One observer stated, "Every hair acted separate from the others." It becomes apparent that, in most respects, work came first for Dmitri Mendeleev.

From his first publication in 1854 entitled "Chemical Analysis of a Sample from Finland" to his final works in 1906 such as "A Project for a School for Teachers" and "Toward Knowledge of Russia", Mendeleev's transcripts revealing his research findings and beliefs number well over 250. His most famous publications include Organic Chemistry, which was published in 1861 when he was 27 years old.

This book won the Domidov Prize and put Mendeleev on the forefront of Russian chemical education. The first edition of Principles of Chemistry was printed in 1868. Both of these books are classroom texts. Again, Mendeleev never lost sight of the importance of education.

Besides his work on general chemical concepts as discussed earlier, Mendeleev spent much of his time working to improve technological advances of Russia. Many of his research findings dealt with agricultural chemistry, oil refining, and mineral recovery.

Dmitri was also one of the founding members of the Russian Chemical Society in 1868, and helped open the lines of communication between scientists in Europe and the United States.

Mendeleev also pursued studies on the properties and behavior of gases at high and low pressures, which led to his development of a very accurate differential barometer and further studies in meteorology. He also became interested in balloons, which led to a rather perilous adventure in 1887.

In order to observe the solar eclipse above Klin, he made a solo ascent, without any prior experience; while his family was rather concerned, he paid no attention to controlling the balloon until after he had completed his observations, at which time he figured out how to land his conveyance.

His greatest accomplishment, however, was the stating of the Periodic Law and the development of the Periodic Table. From early in his career, he felt that there was some type of order to the elements, and he spent more than thirteen years of his life collecting data and assembling the concept, initially with the idea of resolving some of the chaos in the field for his students.

Mendeleev was one of the first modern-day scientists in that he did not rely solely on his own work but rather was in correspondence with scientists around the world in order to receive data that they had collected.

No law of nature, however general , has been established all at once; its recognition has always been preceded by many presentiments. The establishment of a law, moreover, does not take place when the first thought of it takes form, or even when its significance is recognized, but only when it has been confirmed by the results of the experiment. The man of science must consider these results as the only proof of the correctness of his conjectures and opinions.

In 1866, Newlands published a relationship of the elements entitled the "Law of Octaves". Mendeleev's ideas were similar to those of Newlands but Dmitri had more data and felt that Newlands had not gone far enough in his research. By 1869, the Russian chemist had assembled detailed descriptions of more than 60 elements and, on March 6, 1869 a formal presentation was made to the Russian Chemical Society entitled "The Dependence Between the Properties of the Atomic Weights of the Elements." Unfortunately, Mendeleev was ill and the presentation was given by his colleague Professor Menshutken.

EDMOND HALLEY

Edmond Halley was born on October 29, 1656 in Hagerston, Middlesex, England (near London) as son of a wealthy merchant, salter and soapmaker. His birth date is somewhat uncertain because it is not known if at that time in his village the Gregorian or the Julian calendar was in use. There's also some dispute over the year.

He got educated at Oxford and studied at Oxford University, Queen's College, 1673-6. He worked with John Flamsteed, the Astronomer Royal in 1675-6 both at Oxford and Greenwich, and observed e.g. the occultation of Mars by the Moon on August 21, 1676.

In November 1676, he gave up his studies without final exam, and sailed to St. Helena on the southern hemisphere, in order to compile a catalog of southern stars. The reasons for this are unknown, but it may be that he wanted to complement Flamsteed's mapping of the northern celestial hemisphere on the southern skies. Besides compiling this first catalog of the southern skies, Halley observed the Mercury transit of November 7, 1677. After returning to England in 1678, he got his "Catalog of the Southern Stars" published (Halley 1679).

On his return, Halley was elected to the Royal Society on November 30, 1678, and King Charles II graduated him by mandate in 1679. That year, he was sent to Danzig to visit Hevelius.

In the years following, he travelled Europe, urged Isaac Newton to work out and publish his *Principia*, and acquired the expressed enemyship of John Flamsteed. In 1691 Flamsteed succeeded in preventing his appointment as professor in Oxford. In 1704 he was eventually appointed Savilian professor of geometry at Oxford, well to the dismay of Flamsteed.

Halley had observed a number of comets and, following 1695, undertook deep studies to calculate their orbits. In 1705, he published his *"Astronomiae Cometiae Synopsis"*, including his observation that the comet he had observed in 1682 had an orbit almost identical to those of the comets of 1531 and 1607, and concluded these were aparations of one and the same comet, the return of which he predicted for 1758.

In 1710, Halley discovered the proper motion of some "fixed" stars when using Ptolemy's catalog. In 1712, he arranged to publish Flamsteed's observations and star catalogs, an endeavor he had worked on for a long time, heavily opposed by Flamsteed - who later (in 1715) arranged to burn all remaining copies he could get, about 300 of the total edition of 400. In 1715, Halley published a summary of the variable ("New") stars known at that time, six in number (Halley 1715), and in 1716, a summary on the known "nebulae", also six (Halley 1716).

When Flamsteed died, his favorite enemy Halley succeeded him in 1720, then at age 64, and held this position for 21 years.

Halley passed away on January 14, 1742 in Greenwich, England at age 87.

The astronomical community has honored Halley by naming each one crater on Moon (8.0S, 5.7E, 36.0 km diameter, named in 1935) and Mars (48.7S, 59.3W, 84.5 km, in 1973) after him.

Asteroid No. 2688 was named Halley, on its discovery by E. Bowell at Anderson Meșa on April 25, 1982; previously it had been cataloged as 1982 HG1 and former pre-discovery sightings as 1955 QN1 = 1978 SH6 = 1978 TE9 = 1978 UO. But certainly he is best remembered for the comet which he first predicted to return, the most famous of all comets, Comet 1P/Halley.

Halley originally discovered two deepsky objects, globular clusters Omega Centauri (NGC 5139) and the Hercules Cluster, M13. His "Catalog of Southern Stars" (Halley 1679) includes 3 nebulous objects, and he wrote one of the first papers on nebulae, including a catalog of 6 entries/objects (Halley 1716).

EDWARD JENNER

Jenner (1749-1823) was born in Berkeley, England, the third son and youngest of six children of Stephen Jenner, a clergyman of the Church of England. He was orphanedat age five and was raised by his older brother, also a clergyman. When Jenner was thirteen years old, he was apprenticed to a surgeon.

Then in 1770, he moved to London, England, to work with John Hunter (1728-1798), an eminent Scottish anatomist and surgeon who encouraged Jenner to be inquisitive and experimental in his approach to medicine.

Jenner returned to Berkeley in 1773, andset up practice as a country doctor. His curiosity about natural phenomena and dedication to medicine ultimately earned him status as a pioneer of virology and immunology, as well as the founder of the practice of vaccination.

During and prior to Jenner's lifetime, smallpox was a common and often fataldisease worldwide. Many centuries before Jenner's time, the Chinese had begunthe practice of blowing flakes from smallpox scabs up the nostrils of healthy persons to confer immunity to the disease. By the seventeenth century, theTurks and Greeks had discovered that, when injected into the skin of healthyindividuals, the serum from the smallpox pustule induced a mild case of the disease and subsequent immunity.

This practice of inoculation reached Englandby the eighteenth century. However, it was quite risky as those who were inoculated frequently suffered a severe or fatal case of smallpox.

Despite the risk, people willingly agreed to inoculation because of the widespread incidence of smallpox and the fear of suffering from terribly disfiguring pockmarks that resulted from the disease. As a young physician, Jenner noted that dairy workers who had been exposed tocowpox, a disease like smallpox only milder, seemed immune to the more severe infection.

He continually put forth his theory that cowpox could be used toprevent smallpox, but his contemporaries shunned his ideas. They maintainedthat they had seen smallpox victims who claimed to have had earlier cases ofcowpox. It became Jenner's task to transform a country superstition into an acceptedmedical practice. For up until the mid-1770s, the only documented cases of vaccinations using cowpox came from farmers such as Benjamin Jesty of Dorsetshire who vaccinated his family with cowpox using a darning needle.

After observing cases of cowpox and smallpox for a quarter century, Jenner took a step that could have branded him a criminal, just as easily as a hero. On May 14, 1796 he removed the fluid of a cowpox from dairymaid Sarah Nelmes,and inoculated James Phipps, an eight-year-old boy, who soon came down with cowpox. Six weeks later, he inoculated the boy with smallpox. The boy remainedhealthy. Jenner had proved his theory.

He called his method *vaccination*, using the Latin word *vacca*, meaning cow, and *vaccinia*, meaning cowpox. He also introduced the word virus. The publication of Jenner's *An Inquiry into the Causes and Effects of theVariolae Vaccinae* set off an enthusiastic demand for vaccination throughout Europe. Within 18 months, the number of deaths from smallpox had dropped by two-thirds in England after 12,000 people were vaccinated.

By 1800, 100,000peoplc had been vaccinated worldwide. As the demand for the vaccine rapidlyincreased, Jenner discovered that he could take lymph from a smallpox pustuleand dry it in a glass tube for use up to three months later.

The vaccine could then be transported. Jenner was honored and respected throughout Europe and the United States. Athis request, Napoleon released several Englishmen who had been jailed in France in 1804 while France and Great Britain were at war. Across the Atlantic Ocean, Thomas Jefferson received the vaccine from Jenner and proceeded to vaccinate his family and neighbors at Monticello.

However, in his native England,Jenner's medical colleagues refused to allow him entry into the College of Physicians in London, insisting that he first pass a test on the theories of Hippocrates and Galen. Jenner refused to bow to their demands, saying his accomplishments in conquering smallpox should have qualified him for election. Hewas never elected to the college.

Nearly two centuries after Jenner's experimental vaccination of young James,the World Health Organization (WHO) declared smallpox to be eradicated. However, when WHO announced its plan to destroy the last remaining stocks of the smallpox virus (which was used for research) on June 30, 1999, not everyone was pleased with the decision.

Some scientists believe the stockpiled virus could still prove beneficial in terms of research to help fight other deadly viruses, including the human immunodeficiency virus (HIV), which causes AIDS.

FRANK WHITTLE

The British Royal Air Force officer and engineer Sir Frank Whittle (1907-1996) invented the turbojet method of aircraft propulsion. Frank Whittle was born on June 1, 1907, in Coventry, England, the son of a mechanical engineer.

He joined the Royal Air Force as an aircraft apprentice at Cranwell in 1923, where he underwent three years of training as an aircraft mechanic. Then he entered the R.A.F. College at Cranwell as an officer-cadet. Although he was just 21 years old by the time he graduated in 1928, Whittle was already focusing on ways to produce higher speeds and greater altitude for the propellor-driven aircraft of the time.

The title of his final thesis, according to the magazine *Aviation Week & Space Technology*, was *Future Developments in Aircraft Design.* Its theme was a discussion of rocket propulsion and gas turbine-driven propellors, and ways in which they could be used as alternatives to the conventional piston engines then available.

After graduating from Cranwell Whittle became a fighter pilot and was then posted to an instructor's course at the Central Flying School. Here, despite day-to-day responsibilities, he painstakingly designed his first turbojet.

Although sound in theoıy, Whittle's invention was in advance of its time in its material demands, and the Air Ministry rejected it. Nevertheless, he sought patent protection for his invention in 1930 and tried to interest manufacturers in production.

He was granted a patent in 1932, but because of the Great Depression he had little success in finding manufacturers. This was frustrating, but he did not allow this disappointment to interfere with his service career. He attended the Officers' Engineering Course at Henlow (1932-1933) and Cambridge University (1934-1937), where he completed his engineering training while continuing to seek interested investors for his engines. In 1935, having found no factories interested in his engine, he formed his own company together with two partners named Williams and Tinling. Power Jets, Ltd. opened its doors in 1936 and immediately took out further patents with financial backing from O.T. Falk and Company.

By now the Royal Air Force was beginning to take Whittle's work seriously enough to transfer him to the special-duty list, enabling him to continue working on his engine. An experimental version ran in the British Thomson-Houston works at Rugby in April 1937, and by mid-1938 the feasibility of jet propulsion had been established.

After the outbreak of World War II, development of the engine became dependent on Air Ministry finance. However, progress remained slow because of an ambiguous attitude by civil servants toward the unconventional organization of Power Jets, Ltd.

By April 1941 the Gloster Aircraft Company had completed an experimental airframe, and this was fitted with an early Whittle engine for taxiing trials. After an airworthy engine had been fitted, the Gloster-Whittle E28/39 made its first test flight on May 15, 1941.Meanwhile, Whittle did not realize that he had a competitor for his invention in Nazi Germany. Hans von Ohain had not only produced a turbojet, but had also flown it in a Heinkel plane as early as 1939. But though his engine was the first to fly, von Ohain did not have the last word.

Whittle had been generous with his research, sharing his technology with both the British Rolls Royce and the American General Electric Company. His foresight led to renewed interest in both the design of production engines and the airplane which was to become the Gloster *Meteor* twin-engine jet fighter.

In the U.S. collaboration on the development of jet engines with the General Electric Company and the Bell Aircraft Corporation began in September 1941, while Britain was not far behind, putting its *Meteor* aircraft powered by Rolls-Royce "Welland" into service by May 1944.

In 1946 Prime Minister Clement Attlee's Labour government nationalized Whittle's Power Jets company and forced it to limit its activities to components research.

Angrily, Whittle and several coworkers resigned from the company, following up, two years later, with his retirement from the R.A.F. with the rank of Air Commodore, an award of 100,000 pounds, and a knighthood.

In 1976 after several mental breakdowns, Sir Frank emigrated to the U.S. permanently to marry a retired U.S. Navy nurse named Hazel Hall and to take an appointment as a visiting research professor of Aerospace Engineering in the Division of Engineering and Weapons at the U.S. Naval Academy, in Annapolis, Maryland.

He was deep into new research in 1978 when the Federal Aviation Administration decided to honor him by giving him the Extraordinary Service Award, the highest accolade the office can bestow. It was a shining moment in an otherwise quiet appointment, which ended in September 1979.

Whittle was now an elderly man, but he had no intention of fading quietly from view. In 1987 Smithsonian Institution Press published his autobiography, *Whittle, The True Story* which, in a collaboration with John Golley, gave his personal account of the jet engine's development and how it transformed aeronautical design.

Whittle then lived out of the limelight until October 1993, when an article on his achievements appeared in *Aviation Week & Space Technology*. The article's many inaccuracies infuriated him.

Within a month of the magazine's appearance, he presented the editor with a list of 11 corrections, worded with enough military curtness to stress that the 86-year-old author had lost neither his formidable intellect nor his prodigious memory. Although Whittle lived until January, 1996, his letter was his last appearance in print.

GALILEO GALILEI

Galileo remained a devout Catholic throughout his life. "Affiliation: Catholic; It is known to everyone that Galileo was denounced to the Inquisition in 1615 and that he was tried and condemned by the Inquisition in 1633, living the rest of his life under house arrest. All of this was for Copernicanism, not for any heretical theological views."

Additionally, it may be noted that although Galileo himself did not consider his writings about heliocentricity to be heretical, his Catholic leaders at that time did. Today the Catholic Church does not consider heliocentricity or any of Galileo's writings to be heretical.

Galileo is often remembered for his conflict with the Roman Catholic Church. His controversial work on the solar system was published in 1633. It had no proofs of a sun-centered system (Galileo's telescope discoveries did not indicate a moving earth) and his one "proof" based upon the tides was invalid. It ignored the correct elliptical orbits of planets published twenty five years earlier by Kepler.

Since his work finished by putting the Pope's favorite argument in the mouth of the simpleton in the dialogue, the Pope (an old friend of Galileo's) was very offended.

After the "trial" and being forbidden to teach the sun-centered system, Galileo did his most useful theoretical work, which was on dynamics. Galileo expressly said that the Bible cannot err, he saw his system as concerning the issue of how the Bible should be interpreted.

The invention of the telescope and the series of discoveries that resulted from it made Galileo famous. However, by supporting the theory of Copernicus he aroused opposition in important [Catholic] Church circles, and in 1616 he was ordered to refrain from teaching the Copernican hypothesis. Galileo chafed under this restriction for several years.

When the Pope died, in 1623, he was succeeded by a man who had been an admirer of Galileo. The following year the new Pope, Urban VIII, hinted (though somewhat ambiguously) that the prohibition would no longer be in force.

Galileo spent the next six years composing his most famous work, the *Dialogue Concerning the Two Chief World Systems.* This book was a masterly exposition of the evidence in favor of the Copernican theory, and the book was published in 1632 *with* the imprimatur of the Church censors.

Nevertheless, Church authorities responded in anger when the book appeared, and Galileo was soon brought to trial before the Inquisition of Rome on charges of having violated the 1616 prohibition.

It seems clear that many churchmen were unhappy with the decision to prosecute the eminent scientist. Even under the Church law of the time, the case against Galileo was questionable, and he was givena comparitively light sentence. He was not, in fact, confined to jail at all, but merely to house arrest in his own comfortable villa in Arcetri. Theoretically, he was to have no visitors, but that provision of the sentence was not enforced. His only other punishment was the requirement that he publicly recant hs view that the earth moved around the sun.

This the sixty-nine-year-old scientist did in open court. (There is a famous and probably apocryphal story that after he finished making his retraction, Galileo looked down to the earth and whispered softly, "It still moves.") In Arcetri he continued to write on mechanics. He did there, in 1642...

Galileo is probably more responsible than any other man for the empirical attitude of scientific research. It was he who first insisted upon the necessity of performing experiments. He rejected the notion that scientific questions could be decided by reliance upon authority, whether it be the pronouncements of the Church of the assertions of Aristotle.

He also rejected reliance on complex deductive schemes that were not based on a firm foundation of experiment. Medieval scholastics had discussed at great length what *should* happen and *why* things happen, but Galileo insisted upon performing experiments to determine what actually *did* happen. His scientific outlook was distinctly non-mystical; in this respect, he was even more modern than some of his successors, such as Newton.

Galileo, it might be noted, was a deeply religious man. Despite his trial and conviction, he did not reject either religion or the church, but only the attempt of Church authoritie to stifle investigation of scientific matters.

Later generations have quite righlty admired Galileo as a symbol of revolt against dogmatism, and against authoritarian attempts to stifle freedom of thought. Of greater importance, however, is the role he played in founding modern scientific method.

GEORG SIMON OHM

Georg Simon Ohm was born on 16 March 1789 in Erlangen, Bavaria (now Germany). Georg Simon Ohm came from a Protestant family. His father, Johann Wolfgang Ohm, was a locksmith while his mother, Maria Elizabeth Beck, was the daughter of a tailor. Although his parents had not been formally educated, Ohm's father was a rather remarkable man who had educated himself to a high level and was able to give his sons an excellent education through his own teachings.

Had Ohm's brothers and sisters all survived he would have been one of a large family but, as was common in those times, several of the children died in their childhood.

Of the seven children born to Johann and Maria Ohm only three survived, Georg Simon, his brother Martin who went on to become a well-known mathematician, and his sister Elizabeth Barbara.

When they were children, Georg Simon and Martin were taught by their father who brought them to a high standard in mathematics, physics, chemistry and philosophy. This was in stark contrast to their school education. Georg Simon entered Erlangen Gymnasium at the age of eleven but there he received little in the way of scientific training. In fact this formal part of his schooling was uninspired stressing learning by rote and interpreting texts.

This contrasted strongly with the inspired instruction that both Georg Simon and Martin received from their father who brought them to a level in mathematics which led the professor at the University of Erlangen, Karl Christian von Langsdorf, to compare them to the Bernoulli family. It is worth stressing again the remarkable achievement of Johann Wolfgang Ohm, an entirely self-taught man, to have been able to give his sons such a fine mathematical and scientific education.

In 1805 Ohm entered the University of Erlangen but he became rather carried away with student life. Rather than concentrate on his studies he spent much time dancing, ice skating and playing billiards. Ohm's father, angry that his son was wasting the educational opportunity that he himself had never been fortunate enough to experience, demanded that Ohm leave the university after three semesters. Ohm went (or more accurately, was sent) to Switzerland where, in September 1806, he took up a post as a mathematics teacher in a school in Gottstadt bei Nydau.

Karl Christian von Langsdorf left the University of Erlangen in early 1809 to take up a post in the University of Heidelberg and Ohm would have liked to have gone with him to Heidelberg to restart his mathematical studies.

Langsdorf, however, advised Ohm to continue with his studies of mathematics on his own, advising Ohm to read the works of Euler, Laplace and Lacroix. Rather reluctantly Ohm took his advice but he left his teaching post in Gottstadt bei Nydau in March 1809 to become a private tutor in Neuchâtel. For two years he carried out his duties as a tutor while he followed Langsdorf's advice and continued his private study of mathematics. Then in

April 1811 he returned to the University of Erlangen. His private studies had stood him in good stead for he received a doctorate from Erlangen on 25 October 1811 and immediately joined the staff as a mathematics lecturer. After three semesters Ohm gave up his university post. He could not see how he could attain a better status at Erlangen as prospects there were poor while he essentially lived in poverty in the lecturing post. The Bavarian government offered him a post as a teacher of mathematics and physics at a poor quality school in Bamberg and he took up the post there in January 1813.

This was not the successful career envisaged by Ohm and he decided that he would have to show that he was worth much more than a teacher in a poor school. He worked on writing an elementary book on the teaching of geometry while remaining desperately unhappy in his job. After Ohm had endured the school for three years it was closed down in February 1816. The Bavarian government then sent him to an overcrowded school in Bamberg to help out with the mathematics teaching.

On 11 September 1817 Ohm received an offer of the post of teacher of mathematics and physics at the Jesuit Gymnasium of Cologne. This was a better school than any that Ohm had taught in previously and it had a well equipped physics laboratory. As he had done for so much of his life, Ohm continued his private studies reading the texts of the leading French mathematicians Lagrange, Legendre, Laplace, Biot and Poisson.

He moved on to reading the works of Fourier and Fresnel and he began his own experimental work in the school physics laboratory after he had learnt of Oersted's discovery of electromagnetism in 1820. At first his experiments were conducted for his own educational benefit as were the private studies he made of the works of the leading mathematicians.

The Jesuit Gymnasium of Cologne failed to continue to keep up the high standards that it had when Ohm began to work there so, by 1825, he decided that he would try again to attain the job he really wanted, namely a post in a university. Realising that the way into such a post would have to be through research publications, he changed his attitude towards the experimental work he was undertaking and began to systematically work towards the publication of his results:-

Overburdened with students, finding little appreciation for his conscientious efforts, and realising that he would never marry, he turned to science both to prove himself to the world and to have something solid on which to base his petition for a position in a more stimulating environment.

In fact he had already convinced himself of the truth of what we call today "Ohm's law" namely the relationship that the current through most materials is directly proportional to the potential difference applied across the material. The result was not contained in Ohm's firsts paper published in 1825, however, for this paper examines the decrease in the electromagnetic force produced by a wire as the length of the wire increased. The paper deduced mathematical relationships based purely on the experimental evidence that Ohm had tabulated.

In two important papers in 1826, Ohm gave a mathematical description of conduction in circuits modelled on Fourier's study of heat conduction. These papers continue Ohm's deduction of results from experimental evidence and, particularly in the second, he was able to propose laws which went a long way to explaining results of others working on galvanic electricity. The second paper certainly is the first step in a comprehensive theory which Ohm was able to give in his famous book published in the following year.

What is now known as Ohm's law appears in this famous book *Die galvanische Kette, mathematisch bearbeitet* (1827) in which he gave his complete theory of electricity. The book begins with the mathematical background necessary for an understanding of the rest of the work. We should remark here that such a mathematical background was necessary for even the leading German physicists to understand the work, for the emphasis at this time was on a non-mathematical approach to physics. We should also remark that, despite Ohm's attempts in this introduction, he was not really successful in convincing the older German physicists that the mathematical approach was the right one. To some extent, as Caneva explains in, this was Ohm's own fault:-

... in neither the introduction nor the body of the work, which contained the more rigorous development of the theory, did Ohm bring decisively home either the underlying unity of the whole or the connections between fundamental assumptions and major deductions. For example, although his theory was conceived as a strict deductive system based on three fundamental laws, he nowhere indicated precisely which of their several mathematical and verbal expressions he wished to be taken as the canonical form.

It is interesting that Ohm's presents his theory as one of contiguous action, a theory which opposed the concept of action at a distance. Ohm believed that the communication of electricity occurred between "contiguous particles" which is the term Ohm himself uses. The paper is concerned with this idea, and in particular with illustrating the differences in scientific approach between Ohm and that of Fourier and Navier. A detailed study of the conceptual framework used by Ohm in formulating Ohm's law is given in.

As we described above, Ohm was at the Jesuit Gymnasium of Cologne when he began his important publications in 1825. He was given a year off work in which to concentrate on his research beginning in August 1826 and although he only received the less than generous offer of half pay, he was able to spend the year in Berlin working on his publications.

Ohm had believed that his publications would lead to his receiving an offer of a university post before having to return to Cologne but by the time he was due to begin teaching again in September 1827 he was still without such an offer. Although Ohm's work strongly influenced theory, it was received with little enthusiasm. Ohm's feeling were hurt, he decided to remain in Berlin and, in March 1828, he formally resigned his position at Cologne. He took some temporary work teaching mathematics in schools in Berlin. He accepted a position at Nüremberg in 1833 and although this gave him the title of professor, it was still not the university post for which he had strived all his life. His work was eventually recognised by the Royal Society with its award of the Copley Medal in 1841. He became a foreign member of the Royal Society in 1842. Other academies such as those in Berlin and Turin elected him a corresponding member, and in 1845 he became a full member of the Bavarian Academy.

This belated recognition was welcome but there remains the question of why someone who today is a household name for his important contribution struggled for so long to gain acknowledgement.

This may have no simple explanation but rather be the result of a number of different contributary factors. One factor may have been the inwardness of Ohm's character while another was certainly his mathematical approach to topics which at that time were studied in his country a non-mathematical way. There was undoubtedly also personal disputes with the men in power which did Ohm no good at all. He certainly did not find favour with Johannes Schultz who was an influential figure in the ministry of education in Berlin, and with Georg Friedrich Pohl, a professor of physics in that city.

Electricity was not the only topic on which Ohm undertook research, and not the only topic in which he ended up in controversy. In 1843 he stated the fundamental principle of physiological acoustics, concerned with the way in which one hears combination tones. However the assumptions which he made in his mathematical derivation were not totally justified and this resulted in a bitter dispute with the physicist August Seebeck. He succeeded in discrediting Ohm's hypothesis and Ohm had to acknowledge his error. In 1849 Ohm took up a post in Munich as curator of the Bavarian Academy's physical cabinet and began to lecture at the University of Munich.

Only in 1852, two years before his death, did Ohm achieve his lifelong ambition of being appointed to the chair of physics at the University of Munich. Georg Simon Ohm died on 6 July 1854 in Munich, Bavaria, Germany.

GUGLIELMO MARCONI

The Nobel Prize in Physics 1909 Guglielmo Marconi was born at Bologna, Italy, on April 25, 1874, the second son of Giuseppe Marconi, an Italian country gentleman, and Annie Jameson, daughter of Andrew Jameson of Daphne Castle in the County Wexford, Ireland. He was educated privately at Bologna, Florence and Leghorn.

Even as a boy he took a keen interest in physical and electrical science and studied the works of Maxwell, Hertz, Righi, Lodge and others. In 1895 he began laboratory experiments at his father's country estate at Pontecchio where he succeeded in sending wireless signals over a distance of one and a half miles.

In 1896 Marconi took his apparatus to England where he was introduced to Mr. (later Sir) William Preece, Engineer-in-Chief of the Post Office, and later that year was granted the world's first patent for a system of wireless telegraphy.

He demonstrated his system successfully in London, on Salisbury Plain and across the Bristol Channel, and in July 1897 formed The Wireless Telegraph & Signal Company Limited (in 1900 renamed Marconi's Wireless Telegraph Company Limited). In the same year he gave a demonstration to the Italian Government at Spezia where wireless signals were sent over a distance of twelve miles.

In 1899 he established wireless communication between France and England across the English Channel. He erected permanent wireless stations at The Needles, Isle of Wight, at Bournemouth and later at the Haven Hotel, Poole, Dorset.

In 1900 he took out his famous patent No. 7777 for "tuned or syntonic telegraphy" and, on an historic day in December 1901, determined to prove that wireless waves were not affected by the curvature of the Earth, he used his system for transmitting the first wireless signals across the Atlantic between Poldhu, Cornwall, and St. John's, Newfoundland, a distance of 2100 miles.

Between 1902 and 1912 he patented several new inventions. In 1902, during a voyage in the American liner "Philadelphia", he first demonstrated "daylight effect" relative to wireless communication and in the same year patented his magnetic detector which then became the standard wireless receiver for many years.

In December 1902 he transmitted the first complete messages to Poldhu from stations at Glace Bay, Nova Scotia, and later Cape Cod, Massachusetts, these early tests culminating in 1907 in the opening of the first transatlantic commercial service between Glace Bay and Clifden, Ireland, after the first shorter-distance public service of wireless telegraphy had been established between Bari in Italy and Avidari in Montenegro.

In 1905 he patented his horizontal directional aerial and in 1912 a "timed spark" system for generating continuous waves.

In 1914 he was commissioned in the Italian Army as a Lieutenant being later promoted to Captain, and in 1916 transferred to the Navy in the rank of Commander.

He was a member of the Italian Government mission to the United States in 1917 and in 1919 was appointed Italian plenipotentiary delegate to the Paris Peace Conference.

He was awarded the Italian Military Medal in 1919 in recognition of his war service. During his war service in Italy he returned to his investigation of short waves, which he had used in his first experiments.

After further tests by his collaborators in England, an intensive series of trials was conducted in 1923 between experimental installations at the Poldhu Station and in Marconi's yacht "Elettra" cruising in the Atlantic and Mediterranean, and this led to the establishment of the beam system for long distance communication.

Proposals to use this system as a means of Imperial communications were accepted by the British Government and the first beam station, linking England and Canada, was opened in 1926, other stations being added the following year.

In 1931 Marconi began research into the propagation characteristics of still shorter waves, resulting in the opening in 1932 of the world's first microwave radiotelephone link between the Vatican City and the Pope's summer residence at Castel Gandolfo.

Two years later at Sestri Levante he demonstrated his microwave radio beacon for ship navigation and in 1935, again in Italy, gave a practical demonstration of the principles of radar, the coming of which he had first foretold in a lecture to the American Institute of Radio Engineers in New York in 1922.

He has been the recipient of honorary doctorates of several universities and many other international honours and awards, among them the Nobel Prize for Physics, which in 1909 he shared with Professor Karl Braun, the Albert Medal of the Royal Society of Arts, the John Fritz Medal and the Kelvin Medal.

He was decorated by the Tsar of Russia with the Order of St. Anne, the King of Italy created him Commander of the Order of St. Maurice and St. Lazarus, and awarded him the Grand Cross of the Order of the Crown of Italy in 1902.

Marconi also received the freedom of the City of Rome (1903), and was created Chevalier of the Civil Order of Savoy in 1905.

Many other distinctions of this kind followed. In 1914 he was both created a Senatore in the Italian Senate and app ointed Honorary Knight Grand Cross of the Royal Victorian Order in England. He received the hereditary title of Marchese in 1929.

In 1905 he married the Hon. Beatrice O'Brien, daughter of the 14th Baron Inchiquin, the marriage being annulled in 1927, in which year he married the Countess Bezzi-Scali of Rome.

He had one son and two daughters by his first and one daughter by his second wife. His recreations were hunting, cycling and motoring.Marconi died in Rome on July 20, 1937.

HEINRICH RUDOLF HERTZ

Heinrich Rudolf Hertz was born on 22 February, 1857, in Hamburg. His father Dr. jur. Gustav Ferdinand Hertz was Jewish, who had converted to Christianity. He was an advocate in Hamburg, then Oberlandsgerichtsrat, and from 1887 Senator and head of the administration of justice. His mother Anna Elisabeth, née Pfefferkorn, was the daughter of the Frankfurt doctor, Dr. Pfefferkorn.

After attending a private Realschule, Heinrich prepared himself, by private study, for the Johanneum school at which in 1875, after only a year of studying, he passed his school-leaving and university entrance exam Abitur (GCE A-levels), the best in his class. He showed an early interest in the natural sciences, and a practical skill in building physics equipment in the family workshop. He was also an enthusiastic linguist, learning Arabic and Sanskrit.

Then Heinrich Hertz went to Frankfurt to gain practical experience in engineering and after a year of military service with a railway regiment in Berlin (1876-77) he spent a year at the University of Munich.

He had decided on an academic and scientific career rather than one in engineering, and in 1878 chose to continue his studies at the University of Berlin under Gustav Kirchhoff and Hermann von Helmholtz, the foremost physicists of the time. Hertz obtained his Ph.D. degree magna cum laude in 1880 with a thesis on the electromagnetic induction in rotating spheres and continued as Helmholtz's assistant for a further three years.

In 1883 Hertz became a lecturer in theoretical physics at the University of Kiel. With no laboratory facilities at Kiel he had considered more theoretical aspects of physics. Here he began his studies of the recent electromagnetic theory of James Clerk Maxwell. Maxwell's theory had been based on unusual mechanical ideas about the luminiferous ether and had not been universally accepted.

Another scientist, Michelson, assisted by Morley, performed a remarkably clever experiment that proved the non-existence of this ether. In 1884, Hertz rederived Maxwell's equations by a new method, casting them in modern form without assumption of ether.

In 1885, at the age of 28, Heinrich Hertz was appointed professor of physics at the Karlsruhe University. Hertz's early work in Karlsruhe was diverse but included several pieces of research into electrical phenomena and equipment.

Helmholtz had suggested an experimental investigation of the theory to Hertz in 1879, but it was not until 1885 in Karlsruhe that Hertz found the equipment needed for what became his most famous experiments.

In 1886 Hertz married Elizabeth Doll, daughter of a Karlsruhe professor; they had two daughters (Johanna, born on 20.10.1887 and Mathilde, born on 14.01.1891).

It is interesting to note that in 1887 he inadvertently discovered the photoelectric effect whereby ultraviolet radiation releases electrons from the surface of a metal. Although realizing its significance he left others to investigate and explain it.

In 1888, in a corner of his physics classroom at the Karlsruhe Polytechnic in Berlin, Hertz generated electric waves using an electric circuit; the circuit contained a metal rod that had a small gap at its midpoint, and when sparks crossed this gap violent oscillations of high frequency were set up in the rod.

Hertz proved that these waves were transmitted through air by detecting them with another similar circuit some distance away. He also showed that like light waves they were reflected and refracted and, most important, that they traveled at the same speed as light but had a much longer wavelength. Hertz also noted that electrical conductors reflect the waves and that they can be focused by concave reflectors.

He found that nonconductors allow most of the waves to pass through. These waves, originally called Hertzian waves but now known as radio waves, conclusively confirmed Maxwell's prediction on the existence of electromagnetic waves, both in the form of light and radio waves.

In his experiments, Hertz first employed a pair of one meter wires with a spark gap in the center connected to an induction coil as a radiator. The large spheres at the ends were used to adjust the capacity of the circuit for resonance. His receiver was a loop of wire with a small gap across which a small spark could be observed when the radiator discharged.

The receiver was placed several yards from the oscillator. When these rods were given charges of opposite signs, strong enough to spark, the current would oscillate back and forth across the gap and along the rods. With this oscillator, Hertz solved two problems:

1) timing Maxwell's waves (he had demonstrated, in the concrete, what Maxwell had only theorized: that the velocity of radio waves was equal to the velocity of light), and 2) how to make the electric and magnetic fields detach themselves from wires and go free as Maxwell's waves.

Hertz's students were impressed, and wondered what use might be made of this marvelous phenomenon. But Hertz thought his discoveries were no more practical than Maxwell's. "It's of no use whatsoever," he replied. "This is just an experiment that proves Maestro Maxwell was right - we just have these mysterious electromagnetic waves that we cannot see with the naked eye. But they are there." "So, what next?" asked one of his students. Hertz shrugged.

He was a modest man, of no pretensions and, apparently, little ambition. "Nothing, I guess." But, even at a theoretical level, Hertz's accomplishments were quickly seen by others as the beginning of a new "electric age." The English mathematical physicist, Sir. Oliver Heaviside, said in 1891, "Three years ago, electromagnetic waves were nowhere. Shortly afterward, they were everywhere."

Summing up Hertz' experiment importance: his experiments dealing with the reflection, refraction, polarization, interference and velocity of electric waves would trigger the invention, soon after, of the wireless telegraph, radio, television, and radar. It happened this way: in 1888, Hertz described in an electrical journal how he was able to trigger his electromagnetic waves with his oscillator.

A young man in his teens happened to read the article while he was vacationing in the Alps. For him, Hertz's discovery gave him an idea: why not use the waves set off by Hertz's spark oscillator for signaling? Guglielmo Marconi was that young man. He rushed back home to Italy to give the idea a try.

On April 3, 1889, Heinrich Hertz arrived in Bonn to take the position of Professor of Physics and Director of the Physics Institute as successor to Rudolf Clausius (1822–1888). Hertz was fresh from his triumphs in Karlsruhe, where he had proved in a series of elegant experiments that the long-wavelength electromagnetic waves implicit in Maxwell's theory existed.

He also had been able to demonstrate convincingly that these waves had all the well-known properties of light waves – reflection, refraction, interference, polarization. Almost immediately Hertz became the superstar of the physics community, not merely in Germany but throughout the world of science.

But during the almost five years that Hertz spent in Bonn (April 3, 1889, to January 1, 1894), he abandoned almost all experimental work and devoted three years to difficult theoretical work on mechanics, which culminated in the posthumous publication in 1894 of his book on the subject.

(Heinrich Hertz, Die Prinzipien der Mechanik in neuem Zusammenhange dargestellt, Philipp Lenard (Ed.), Leipzig: J.A. Barth, 1894; translated by D.E. Jones, J. T. Walley, The Principles of Mechanics Presented in a New Form, London: Macmillan and Co., 1899; reprinted New York: Dover Publications, 1956.)

Why, in his hour of triumph, did Hertz turn his back on electromagnetic experiments (after completing one that he had begun in Karlsruhe), and devote three years to this book on mechanics, a book that always has mystified physicists?

A practical reason (but certainly not the dominant one) is that he was increasingly ill with a series of infections during these years, and thus was unable to do the laboratory research he found so rewarding both personally and professionally. He also found it difficult to find new experimental projects that promised to rival his Karlsruhe research in importance.

The salient reason for his work on theoretical mechanics, however, was that as a nineteenth-century physicist, like most such physicists, Hertz firmly maintained that the ultimate goal of physics was to reduce all observable physical phenomena to mechanics.

In addition to his theoretical studies in mechancs, Hertz performed research on the discharge of electricity in rarefied gases. Hertz also continued his analysis of Maxwell's theory, publishing two papers in 1890.

His experimental and theoretical work put the field of electrodynamics on a much firmer footing. His scientific papers were translated into English and published in three volumes:

Electric Waves (1893), Miscellaneous Papers (1896), and Principles of Mechanics (1899).

Hertz suffered from a bone disease during Summer 1892. Heinrich Hertz died of blood poisoning on 1 January 1894 in Bonn, when not quite 37. His tragic early death occurred after several years of poor health and cut short a brilliant career. He is buried in the Jewish cemetery in Ohlsdorf, Hamburg, Germany.

ISAAC NEWTON

Newton was born into the Anglican church and publicly conformed to it. At about age 30 he came to believe "that Trinitarianism was a fraud and that Arianism was the true form of primitive Christianity. Newton held these views, very privately, until the end of his life. On his death bed he refused to receive the sacrament of the Anglican church."

Newton died in 1727, and was buried in Westminster Abbey [an Anglican church], the first scientist to be accorded that honor.

In optics, mechanics, and mathematics, Newton was a figure of undisputed genius and innovation. In all his science (including chemistry) he saw mathematics and numbers as central.

What is less well known is that he was devoutly religious and saw numbers as involved in understanding from the Bible God's plan for history. He did a lot of work on biblical numerology, and, though aspects of his beliefs were not orthodox, he thought theology very important. In his system of physics, God is essential to the nature and absoluteness of space.

In *Principia* he stated, "The most beautiful system of the sun, planets, and comets, could only proceed from the counsel and dominion on an intelligent and powerful Being."

Isaac Newton... was devoutly religious in his search for God, puritanical in his morality, abstemious, scrupulous, austere, loveless and joyless. Nevertheless, his prestige forged a permanent link between science and government.

Newton's masterpiece was in theoretical physics, *Philosophiae Naturalis Principia Mathematica* (1687), an intellectual monument to mankind, a synthesis of grandeur... He established mathematical physics, e.g., fluid dynamics and acoustics. *The Principia* was written in Latin, its proofs were geometrical, despite his having invented fluxions, a form of calculus. On the contrary, the *Opticks* (1704) was written in English with experimental queries...

The young Newton did not aspire to ecclesiastical orders requisite for the mastership of a college. His theological interests, however, were not an aberration of old age. All his life he was a conforming member of the Anglican Church, although he had reservations about its Trinitarian doctrine.

Although he appreciated its universalist humanitarianism, he was by no means a deist inasmuch as he believed in a personal God, omniscient and omnipotent, but, above all, immanent not only had He created the universe, but He keeps it under constant surveillance and intervenes in a providential way from time to time (e.g., paths of comets).

Neither was Newton a Unitarian; he believed in Jesus Christ as the Messiah, the Son of God-not a mere man, but a sort of viceroy for the Father (his precise concept is somewhat problematic). Newton diligently sought the Creator through His actions, His work (creation) and His Word (the Bible). (Newton probably kept his non-orthodox views secret to refrain from disruptive controversies in the church.)

Newton believed in past miracles ("the sun standing still," however, he regarded as a poetic expression: Moses as a popularizer) and prophecies — no longer needed. In general, he interpreted the Bible literally. (Among his effects upon death was a well-worn Bible (1660) — now lost.) He performed meticulous exegesis of the Scriptures.

He regarded Church history as of primary importance for understanding Christianity. An assiduous reader and an erudite historian (he knew Greek, Hebrew, and Latin), he examined scores of texts for corruptions and misinterpretations. His vehement anti-Catholicism stemmed from the initially political endorsement of Athanasius' creed and from the later biblical mistranslation by Jerome.

He himself was convinced by the argument from design in its major features, not in minutiae; possibly a mystic in connection with his alchemical investigations, he always relied upon facts per se. Newton was a critical historian for his time, but he did have a fanatical belief in the writings of antiquity (e.g., a crucial fragment of Eudoxus).

He was particularly attracted to the prophetic records of Daniel and St. John the Divine, which he regarded in agreement in the smallest detail. (Biblical prophecies, he felt, can be understood only ex post facto.)

Newton's historical interests engaged his attention more than fifty years; his extant writings along this line are esoteric and scattered among numerous manuscripts. *The Chronology of Ancient Kingdoms Amended* and *Observations upon the Prophecies of Daniel and the Apocalyse of St. John* were published posthumously (1728). Together, in the accepted historical method of that time, they provide a chronology of world history, sacred and profane.

Both the Principia and the Optics close with affirmations about God; the famous "Scholium" of the former is a passionate statement about the creation. As our idea of the universe expands, so, too, does our concept of God.

Newton was wholeheartedly committed to the commandments of the Bible (O.T. and N.T.)-in an absolute sense. Unfortunately, he envisaged God more as a just ruler than a Father of grace, love, and mercy. He lacked emotion, although he did record 58 sins about Whitsunday when he was 19. He minimized ritual, as well as dogma. (He did not seek the last rites of the Church.)

He noted that there were many rites among the early Christians, but only one faith. Although the Royal Society had many divines as members, in the spirit of Francis Bacon, it barred any public discussion of politics and of religion-presumably for the sake of unity. Privately, however, Newton recognized that we all live in one world, our Father's world.

He regarded religion and science as interrelated; science, indeed, the handmaiden of religion, its Te Deum-hence no fundamental conflict. In both he insisted upon a common mental approach, a foundation of facts, historical and natural.

He corrected the death date (34) of Christ, and that of the Argonaut's search (956) and hence of Troy's fall, 904 (both about 3 centuries late by modern standards). His application of astronomical dating (eclipses, equinoctial precession, et at.) was revolutionary. He was, however, very much opposed to metaphysicians such as Descartes and Leibnitz, both in science and in theology. He looked upon history and nature as similar in that they both have latent secrets, both being actually simple and measurable.

Newton's whole life was dominated by religion, his search for the Creator of heaven and earth. Toward the end of his life he mused, "I do not know what I may appear to the world; but to myself I appear to have been but a little boy, playing on the sea-shore, and diverting myself, in now and then finding a smooth pebble or a prettier shell than ordinary, whilst the great ocean of truth lay all undiscovered before me."

JAGADISH CHANDRA BOSE

Sir Jagadish Chandra Bose (November 30, 1858 – November 23, 1937) was a Bengali polymath: a physicist, biologist, botanist, archaeologist, and science fiction writer. He pioneered the investigation of radio and microwave optics, made extremely significant contributions to plant science, and laid the foundations of experimental science in the Indian subcontinent.

He is considered the father of radio science, and is also considered the father of Bengali science fiction. He was the first from the Indian subcontinent to get a US patent, in 1904.

Born in Bengal province of British India, Bose completed graduation from St. Xavier's College, Calcutta. Then he went to the University of London to study medicine, but couldn't complete his study due to health problems.

He returned to India and joined the Presidency College as a Professor of Physics. There, in spite of racial discrimination, and lack of funding and equipment, Bose carried on his scientific research. He made remarkable progress in his research of remote wireless signaling and was the first to use semiconductor junction to detect radio signals. However, instead of trying to gain commercial benefit from this invention Bose made his inventions public in order to allow others to develop on his research. Subsequently he made some pioneering discoveries in plant physiology.

He used his own invention crescograph to measure plant response to various stimuli, and thereby scientifically proved parallelism between animal and plant tissues. Although Bose filed for patent for one of his inventions due to peer pressure his reluctance to any form of patenting was well known. Now about 70 years of after his death he is being credited for many of his contributions to modern science.

Bose returned to India in 1885, carrying a letter from Fawcett, the economist to Lord Ripon, Viceroy of India. On Lord Ripon's request Sir Alfred Croft, the Director of Public Instruction, appointed Bose officiating professor of physics in Presidency College. The principal C.H.Tawney protested against the appointment but had to accept it.

Bose was not provided with facilities for research. On the other hand, he was 'victim of racialism' with regard to his salary. In those days, an Indian professor was paid Rs. 200 per month, while an European drew Rs. 300 per month. Since Bose was officiating, he was offered a salary of only Rs. 100 per month.

With remarkable sense of self respect and national pride he decided on a new form of protest. Bose refused to accept the salary cheque. In fact, he continued his teaching assignment for three years without salary.

Finally both the Director of Public Instruction and the Principal of the Presidency College fully realised the value of Bose's skill in teaching and also his lofty character. As a result his appointment was made permanent with retrospective effect. He was given the full salary for the previous three years in lumpsum.

Presidency College lacked a proper laboratory. Bose had to conduct his researches in a small 24 square foot room. He devised equipments for the research with the help of one untrained tinsmith. Sister Nivedita writes, "I was horrified to find the way in which a great worker could be subjected to continuous annoyance and petty difficulties.

The college routine was made as arduous as possible for him, so that he could not have the time he needed for investigation." After his daily grind, which he of course performed with great conscientiousness, he carried out his research far into the night, in a small room in his college.

Moreover, the policy of the British government for its colonies was not conducive to attempts at original research. Bose spent his hard-earned money for making experimental equipment. Within a decade of his joining Presidency College, he emerged a pioneer in the incipient research field of wireless waves.

In 1887, Bose married Abala, daughter of the renowned Brahmo reformer Durga Mohan Das. Abala was awarded Bengal government scholarship in 1882 to study medicine in Madras (now Chennai), but had to give up because of ill health.

At the time of their marriage Bose was facing financial crisis due to not drawing salaries and some debts of his father. The newly married couple faced privations and came out with flying colours, repaying the debts of Bose's father. Bose's parents lived for sometime after the debts were cleared.

The British theoretical physicist James Clerk Maxwell mathematically predicted the existence of electromagnetic waves of diverse wavelengths, but he died in 1879 before his prediction was experimentally verified. British physicist Oliver Lodge demonstrated the existence of Maxwell's waves transmitted along wires in 1887-88.

The German physicist Heinrich Hertz showed experimentally, in 1888, the existence of electromagnetic waves in free space. Subsequently, Lodge pursued Hertz's work and delivered a commemorative lecture in June 1894 (after Hertz's death) and published it in book form. Lodge's work caught the attention of scientists in different countries including Bose in India.

The first remarkable aspect of Bose's follow up microwave research was that he reduced the waves to the millimetre level (about 5 mm wavelength). He knew that long waves were advantageous because of their great penetrative power but realised their disadvantages for studying the light like-properties of those electric waves.

In November 1894 (or in 1895) in a public demonstration in Kolkata, Bose ignited gunpowder and rang a bell at a distance using millimetre range wavelength microwaves. The demonstration was held in the Town Hall of Calcutta, in the presence of Sir William Mackenzie, the Lieutenant Governor, and Bose wrote in a Bengali essay, *Adrisya Alok* {Invisible Light),

"The invisible light can easily pass through brick walls, buildings etc. Therefore, messages can be transmitted by means of it without the mediation of wires." This was one year after Nikola Tesla made the first public demonstration of radio communication in 1893. In Russia, Popov was performing similar experiments, but had recorded in December 1895 that he was hoping for distant signalling with radio waves.

Bose's first scientific paper, "On polarisation of electric rays by double-refracting crystals" was communicated to the Asiatic Society of Bengal in May 1895, within a year of Lodge's paper. His second paper was communicated to the Royal Society of London by Lord Rayleigh in October 1895.

In December 1895, the London journal the *Electrician* (Vol 36) published Bose's paper, "On a new electro-polariscope". At that time, the word 'coherer', coined by Lodge, was used in the English-speaking world for Hertzian wave receivers or detectors. The *Electrician* readily commented on Bose's coherer. (December 1895). *The Englishman* (18 January 1896) quoted from the *Electrician* and commented as follows:

"Should Professor Bose succeed in perfecting and patenting his 'Coherer', we may in time see the whole system of coast lighting throughout the navigable world revolutionised by a Bengali scientist working single handed in our Presidency College Laboratory."

Bose planned to "perfect his coherer" but never thought of patenting it. The 1895 public demonstration by Bose in Kolkata was before Marconi's wireless signalling experiment on Salisbury Plain in England in May 1897.

Bose went to London on a lecture tour in 1896 and met Marconi, who was conducting wireless experiments for the British post office. In an interview, Bose said he was not interested in commercial telegraphy and others can use his research work.

In 1899, Bose announced the development of a "*iron-mercury-iron coherer with telephone detector*" in a paper presented at the Royal Society, London.

It appears that Bose's demonstration of remote wireless signalling has priority over Marconi. He was the first to use a semiconductor junction to detect radio waves, and he invented various now commonplace microwave components. In 1954 Pearson and Brattain gave priority to Bose for the use of a semi-conducting crystal as a detector of radio waves.

Further work at millimetre wavelengths was almost nonexistent for nearly 50 years. Just one hundred years ago, Bose described to the Royal Institution in London his research carried out in Kolkata at millimetre wavelengths.

He used waveguides, horn antennas, dielectric lenses, various polarisers and even semiconductors at frequencies as high as 60 GHz; much of his original equipment is still in existence, now at the Bose Institute in Kolkata.

Concepts from his original 1897 papers have been incorporated into a new 1.3 mm multi-beam receiver now in use on the NRAO 12 Metre Telescope, Arizona, U.S.A. Neville Francis Mott, Nobel

Laureate in 1977 for his own contributions to solid-state electronics, remarked that "J.C. Bose was at least 60 years ahead of his time" and "In fact, he had anticipated the existence of P-type and N-type semiconductors."

His next contribution to science was in plant physiology. He forwarded a theory for the ascent of sap in plants in 1927, his theory contributed to the vital theory of ascent of sap. According to his theory, electromechanical pulsations of living cells were responsible for the ascent of sap in plants.

He was skeptical about the then, and still now, most popular theory for the ascent of sap, the tension-cohesion theory of Dixon and Joly, first proposed in 1894.

The 'CP theory', proposed by Canny in 1995, validates this skepticism. Canny experimentally demonstrated pumping in the living cells in the junction of the endodermis.

In his research in plant stimuli, he showed with the help of his newly invented crescograph that plants responded to various stimuli as if they had nervous systems like that of animals.

He therefore found a parallelism between animal and plant tissues. His experiments showed that plants grow faster in pleasant music and its growth retards in noise or harsh sound. This was experimentally verified later on.

His major contribution in the field of biophysics was the demonstration of the electrical nature of the conduction of various stimuli (wounds, chemical agents) in plants, which were earlier thought to be of chemical in nature. These claims were experimentally proved by *Wildon et al* (Nature, 1992, 360, 62–65).

He also studied for the first time action of microwaves in plant tissues and corresponding changes in the cell membrane potential, mechanism of effect of seasons in plants, effect of chemical inhibitor on plant stimuli, effect of temperature etc.

He claimed that plants can "feel pain, understand affection etc.," from the analysis of the nature of variation of the cell membrane potential of plants, under different circumstances. According to him a plant treated with care and affection gives out a different vibration compared to a plant subjected to torture.

JAMES CLERK MAXWELL

James Clerk Maxwell: Devout Protestant Christian. "Maxwell's breadth of appreciation of Christianity grew still further during his time in London. To his background of Presbyterianism (in the Scottish kirk of his father's tradition) and the Anglicanism of his mother and Cambridge, he added an experience of the Baptists."

Home educated in a remote region of Scotland, Maxwell showed early signs of brilliance... Edinburgh University accepted Maxwell when he was sixteen... Faculty members soon urged Maxwell to transfer to Cambridge where superior equipment was available. He first needed to obtain the consent of his father, John Maxwell, who had fostered his son's education at every turn...

The elder Maxwell was reluctant to accede, having hoped to make a lawyer of his son. He also feared that in the less fervent English church, James would lapse from his Christian upbringing. But in the end, ye yielded to his son's pleas...

James Clerk Maxwell's free lectures, given under the auspices of Frederick Denison Maurice's Christian outreach (the Christian socialist Maurice founded two colleges for poor working men), were well attended by the working poor... he visited Europe, where he found ready entrance into the scientific establishments of the day.

Outside France he was quarantined on a ship with sick passengers, the authorities suspecting plague.He insisted on personally nursing the ill as his Christian duty...

Cancer... infected his abdomen. Despite intense pain he continued work up to his own death at forty-eight. Almost his last words were "God help my poor wife." *Science* magazine eulogized him, reminding the readers of Maxwell's well-known Christian convictions; in him there was a profound mystical strain, although he spoke little of it publicly. In his view, scientists should not trumpet the religious implications of their findings.

He believed that Lord Kelvin, Buckland, Sedgwick, and others had embarrassed themselves by doing just that when many of their conclusions proved premature. Nonetheless, Maxwell was noted for his extemporaneous prayers, of which we have at least one recorded example:

"Teach us to study the works of Thy hands that we may subdue the earth to our use and strengthen our reason for Thy service." In a letter to his wife he mused that the scientist in union with Christ has an obligation to do such work as will benefit the body of Christ.

James Clerk Maxwell (1831-79), born in Edinburgh, was the son of a Scottish Laird, an advocate, whose small farm-estate was called Glenlair... Having received a B.A. in 1854 he obtained a fellowship at Trinity the next year...

He died at the early age of thirty-eight. This brilliant scientist was buried in the churchyard of the Parton Kirk, where he had been an elder...

There was a single-heartedness to Maxwell, a depth of unity in his life as a whole, a unity of his nature. He exhibited not only scientific industriousness, but also basic poetic feeling and imagination.

He was profoundly sincere. At the same time he had an overflowing humor; there was elasticity in his step, a sparkle in his eye.

He was an avid reader, particularly of English literature. It was said there was "not a single subject on which he cannot talk and talk well." He had a retentive memory and a facility for versification. His marriage to Katherine M. Dewar, daughter of the Principal of Marischal, was a happy one; together they read the English classics.

He was devoted to her; his dying glance was fixed on her-a sort of mystical marriage. He rode with her; he walked with his dog. He had a tenderness for all living things.

Maxwell had an extensive and minute knowledge of the Scriptures from his childhood. It is said that he knew the chapter and verse of almost any quotation from the Psalms (by age eight he had memorized Ps. 119). As a schoolboy he had attended St. Andrews Sunday mornings and the Episcopal Chapel in the afternoons.

Although his hereditary piety and historical interest was in Calvinism, he never identified himself with any particular religious opinion. He had an innate reverence for sacred things. To be sure, he had an interest in things more than in people, in theology more than in anthropology.

In him there was a blending of Presbyterian and Episcopalian. He read and thought much on religious subjects. Although orthodox, he was tolerant of unbelievers such as WK. Clifford. A favorite book was Thomas Browne's "Religio Medici"; a favorite author, George Herbert.

"There was deep humility before his God, reverent submission to His will, and hearty belief in the love and atonement of that Divine Saviour." He was a regular communicant at the College Chapel, regular in his church attendance, charitable.

At Glenlair he would visit the sick, read and pray with them. There were daily prayers in his household. For example, "Teach us to study the work of Thy hands that we may subdue the earth to our uses, and strengthen our reason for Thy service; and so rescue Thy blessed Word, that we may believe on Him whom Thou hast sent to give us the knowledge of salvation and the remission of our sins."

In 1875 he remarked, "I think that men of science as well as other men need to learn from Christ, and I think that Christians whose minds are scientific are bound to study science that this view of the glory of God may be as extensive as their being is capable of."

In his early twenties he had noted, "Happy is the man who can recognize in the work of Today a connected portion of the work of life, and an embodiment of the work of Eternity."

Finally, at twenty-seven he had concluded, "The more we enter into Christ's work He will have more room to work His work in us. For He always desires us to be one with us. Our worship is social, and Christ will be where two or three are gathered together in His name."

JOHANNES KEPLER

Kepler was a brilliant mathematician and astronomer. He did early work on light, and established the laws of planetary motion about the sun. He also came close to reaching the Newtonian concept of universal gravity - well before Newton was born!

His introduction of the idea of force in astronomy changed it radically in a modern direction. Kepler was an extremely sincere and pious Lutheran, whose works on astronomy contain writings about how space and the heavenly bodies represent the Trinity. Kepler suffered no persecution for his open avowal of the sun-centered system, and, indeed, was allowed as a Protestant to stay in Catholic Graz as a Professor (1595-1600) when other Protestants had been expelled!

The founder of modern astronomy... His real dream was to enter the ministry, but economic necessity forced him to pursue mathematics. He would later recognize God's leading in the academic route he followed... Harrassment over his religious beliefs compelled him to leave Gratz [Austria] in 1597. He spent some time in Prague, but community opposition to his Lutheranism eventually drove him from there as well. The persecution led him to his big break. Kepler began working with Tycho Brahe...

All of Kepler's writings and letters displayed deep religious convictions. He held that Scripture used the common expressions of mankind when it spoke about mundane things as opposed to spiritual mattes.

Hence, he perceived the Bible to be a spiritual and not a scientific guide. He held reason to be above authority in matters of natural philosophy, while authority (that is, church and Scripture) ruled in matters of religion.

Beneath it all, he saw himself as a priset of nature whose discoveries glorified the name of God. Firmly believing that God created the universe, Kepler sought to discover how it was set in motion. "I wanted to become a theologian," he wrote. "For a long time I was restless.

Now, however, behold how through my effort God is being celebrated in astronomy." As a Lutheran working in areas controlled by Catholics, he suffered pangs of conscience when forced to make compromises.

When *Mysterium cosmographicum* was printed, Kepler's school requested he delte passages referring to Scripture. He did so, but in a short tract explained his view on the relationship of Scripture to science. Unfortunately, Galileo borrowed from it freely and without attribution so that it came to be reprinted as his own work.

Johannes Kepler (1571-1630) was a rare and strange man whose life was fraught with vicissitudes stemming from the Diet of Augsburg (155 5) with its principle "cuius regio, eius religio" to the devastating Thirty Years War (1618-1648). He was born of Lutheran parents (father a soldier, mother daughter of an innkeeper) in Weil der Stadt, Wfirttemberg.

At seven he was sent to a cloister Latin school and at thirteen to a seminary, from which he received a B.A. Two years later he was awarded an M.A. from the protestant University of TUbingen, which he had entered at eighteen to become a Lutheran priest. In the middle of the third year of his subsequent theological preparation the faculty recommended him to be teacher of mathematics and astronomy at the protestant seminary in Graz, Austria, where he was also appointed District Mathematician. (He married at twenty-six.)

At twenty-eight he met the Danish astronomer Tycho Brahe (1546-1601) at Prague. Not being a Catholic, he was banished the following year. At thirty he began collaborating with Brahe on the Rudolphine Tables. In that very year, however, Brahe died; Rudolph 11 appointed Kepler to succeed him as Imperial Mathematician. Only his wife's income saved him from the embarassment of uncertain salary payments.

Upon the Emperor's forced abdication in 1612 and his own refusal to become a Catholic, he had to seek employment elsewhere again, this time as District Mathematician in Linz. (His wife having died, he remarried-a happier venture.)... His outstanding characteristic, however, was his integrity resulting in sincere and frank behaviour. He was conscientious; agreeing with the new Gregorian calendar (1582), he did not side with the protestant opposition, which lasted until about 1700.

Despite his personal political problems he never resorted to religious agitation; he was always urging peace. Himself modest, he recommended that jealous observers share their observations of an eclipse. He had a noble spirit; he was deeply religious...

A Platonist, Kepler was a mathematical mystic. He believed that "everything in nature is arranged according to measure and number." He was convinced that "the geometrical natures of things have provided the Creator the model for decorating the whole world." (He investigated the regularity of the six angles of a snowflake in "Strena" (1611), His axiom was that "nothing in the world was created by God without a plan"; he sought it diligently.

Kepler's official duties included preparation of ephemerides and calendars, involving weather predictions and astrological notes.

He was the first to place the birth of Jesus at 4 B.C... As for any influences of the stars, he exercised restraint and caution — he recognized their general psychic effects, but avoided specific predictions. He seized the opportunity to give moral admonitions, to urge peaceful practices.

Kepler wrote occasional papers on theology, but he never claimed to be a theologian. He regarded himself as a layman who was a mathematician, a (natural) philosopher, a historian. And yet, he was probably the scientist who par excellence regarded science and religion as different aspects of an integrated world-not an artificial, academic bifurcation.

The goal of science, he believed, is to bring man to God; the principle of his scientific work is praise of God. "We astronomers are priests of the highest God in regard to the book of nature." "God is the beginning and end of scientific research and striving"-the keynote of his thought, the basis of his purpose, the "life-giving soil of his feeling." For him, "geometry is unique and eternal, a reflection of the mind of God. That mankind shows in it is because man is an image of God."

Kepler regarded the Copernican theory as literally true — not a convenient fiction. With respect to questionable Biblical passages, he noted, "It is not the purpose of the Holy Scriptures to instruct men in natural things." Despite his exemplary life, he was denied communion by his own Lutheran church, first at Graz, finally by Tffbingen in answer to his formal petition.

Although he subscribed wholeheartedly to the Augsburg Confession, he could not quite endorse the Book of Concord (1580) because of its doctrine of the omnipresence of Christ (e.g., in the sacrament).

He preferred the Calvinistic emphasis upon remembrance, but could not accept its complementary insistence upon predestination. He regarded himself as a catholic (including

Lutherans and Calvinists, as well as Roman Catholics), but he could not agree with the Papacy.

Kepler's scientific writings are interspersed with pertinent religious comments. The "Harmonices," his favorite work, begins and ends with an appropriate prayer, (it contains also explanations about Jesus Christ).

The conclusion begins, "0 Thou, who by the light of nature increases in us the desire for the light of Thy mercy in order to be led by this to Thy glory, to Thee I offer thanks, Creator, God, because Thou hast given me pleasure in what Thou hast created and I rejoice in Thy handiwork."

His dying words were: "Only the merits of our saviour Jesus Christ. It is in Him, as I steadfastly testify, that there rest all my retreat, all my consolation, all my hope."

JOSEPH HENRY

Joseph Henry (1797-1878), the leading American scientist after Benjamin Franklin until Willard Gibbs, was a professor at Princeton from 1832 to 1846. His chief scientific contributions were in the field of electromagnetism, where he discovered the phenomenon of self-inductance.

The unit of inductance, called "the henry," immortalizes his name. Henry is also remembered as the first Secretary of the Smithsonian Institution, where he made extraordinary contributions to the organization and development of American science.

Of Scottish descent, Henry was the son of a day-laborer in Albany, N.Y. As a small boy he was sent to live with his grandmother in a village about 40 miles from Albany. There he worked in a general store after school hours and at the age of thirteen was apprenticed to a watchmaker.

As a young man he became interested in the theater and was offered employment as a professional actor, but in 1819 several well-positioned Albany friends persuaded him instead to attend the Albany Academy, where free tuition was provided. His interest in science had already been aroused by a chance encounter with a popular scientific book, and by 1823 his education was so far advanced that he was assisting in the teaching of science courses.

By 1826, after a stint as a district schoolteacher and as a private tutor, he was appointed Professor of Mathematics and Natural Philosophy at the Academy. Here, in spite of a teaching schedule that occupied him seven hours a day, he did his most important scientific experiments.

Henry had become interested in terrestrial magnetism, which was then, as today, an important scientific topic. This led him to experiment with electromagnetism. His apprenticeship as a watchmaker stood him in good stead in the construction of batteries and other apparatus. Oersted and others had observed magnetic effects from electric currents, but Henry was the first to wind insulated wires around an iron core to obtain powerful electromagnets.

Before he left Albany, he built one for Yale that would lift 2,300 pounds, the largest in the world at that time. In experimenting with such magnets, Henry observed the large spark that was generated when the circuit was broken, and he deduced the property known as self-inductance, the inertial characteristic of an electric circuit.

The self-inductance of a circuit tends to prevent the current from changing; if a current is flowing, self-inductance tends to keep it flowing, or if an electromotive force is applied self-inductance tends to keep it from building up.

Henry found that the self-inductance is greatly affected by the configuration of the circuit, especially the coiling of the wire. He also discovered how to make non-inductive windings by folding the wire back on itself.

While Henry was doing these experiments, Michael Faraday did similar work in England. Henry was always slow in publishing his results, and he was unaware of Faraday's work. Today Faraday is recognized as the discoverer of mutual inductance (the basis of transformers), while Henry is credited with the discovery of self-inductance.

In 1832, when Henry was 35, Yale's distinguished geologist Benjamin Silliman was consulted regarding the possible appointment of Henry to Princeton. Silliman replied, "As a physical philosopher he has no superior in our country; certainly not among the young men." Henry, always modest, had responded to tentative inquiries, "Are you aware of the fact that I am not a graduate of any college and that I am principally self-educated?"

Henry's initial salary at Princeton was $1,000 per annum plus a house. The Trustees also provided $100 "for the purchase of a new electrical machine &c." At that point the College was near bankruptcy and Maclean was trying to institute reforms and build up the faculty. Henry was a notable acquisition, and he found the lighter teaching schedule and the intellectual companionship at Princeton congenial, especially when his brother-in-law Stephen Alexander joined the faculty to teach astronomy.

Henry worked with Alexander in the observation of sunspots and continued his own work on magnets, building for Princeton an even larger magnet than he had built for Yale, one that would lift 3,500 pounds. He also rigged two long wires, one in front of Nassau Hall and one behind, so that he was able to send a signal by induction through the building.

Another wire from his laboratory in Philosophical Hall to his home on the campus was used to send signals to his wife; this signal system used a remote electromagnet to close a switch for a stronger local circuit, and constituted in effect the invention of the magnetic relay.

A similar arrangement was used by S.F.B. Morse in the invention of the telegraph; Morse had consulted Henry and had used one of his scientific papers. Later, Henry was called to testify in a patent suit involving the telegraph, *Morse* vs. *O'Reilly.* Although Henry had encouraged and helped Morse in his project, his testimony that the principle of the telegraph had been known to himself and to Professor Wheatstone in England undermined Morse's claim to originality. This led to much unpleasantness and controversy, but Henry's reputation emerged unscathed.

In addition to natural philosophy (physics), Henry taught chemistry, geology, mineralogy, astronomy, and architecture — in the words of Frederick Seitz, Ph.D. '34, former president of the National Academy of Sciences, he was "a very large economy package." A rather reserved and quiet man, he was nevertheless a popular teacher.

The College gave Henry an opportunity, then unusual, to travel abroad on leave at full salary. In 1837 he met Faraday, Wheatstone, and other British scientists, to whom he explained his idea of "quantity" and "intensity" circuits (low and high impedance, in modern terms). He returned to Princeton with a variety of scientific equipment purchased abroad.

During his remaining years in Princeton Henry continued his electrical investigations, but also branched out into the study of phosphorescence, sound, capillary action, and ballistics. In 1844 he was a member of a committee to investigate the explosion of a gun during a demonstration on the new U.S.S. *Princeton*; the Secretaries of State and Navy and several congressmen were among the spectators killed. His experiments on gun castings on this committee led him into the subject of the molecular cohesion of matter.

In 1846, having received from an Englishman, James Smithson, a large bequest for the founding of an institution "for the increase and diffusion of knowledge among men," the U.S. Congress established the Smithsonian Institution. A distinguished board was appointed, with instructions to find the best possible man to head the new Institution as secretary, and the invitation was soon extended to Henry.

He was reluctant to leave Princeton and the opportunity to do his own scientific investigations. "If I go," he said to a friend, "I shall probably exchange permanent fame for transient reputation."

But he finally accepted and threw his enormous energy and knowledge and experience into the development of the Smithsonian, which became the first great driving force in the organization and direction of American science.

Henry was one of the original members of the National Academy of Sciences and served as its second president. He was also a trustee of Princeton and president of the American Association for the Advancement of Science.

When he died in 1878 his funeral was attended by the president of the United States with his cabinet, the chief justice and associate justices of the Supreme Court, by many members of both houses of Congress, and by many scientists and other illustrious personages.

In 1872, John C. Green, founder of the School of Science at Princeton, endowed a chair of physics in Henry's honor (held since then by C. F. Brackett, W. F. Magie, E. P. Adams, H. D. Smyth, and J. A. Wheeler).

Almost a century later, when the main physics building, Jadwin Hall, was dedicated in 1970, the Physics Department manifested its continuing esteem for Henry by declaring that all of the laboratory facilities housed in Jadwin and Palmer Halls and the Elementary Particles Laboratory should be collectively known as the Joseph Henry Laboratories.

Some of Henry's laboratory equipment is on display in the lobby of Jadwin Hall. His campus home, built to his design, is called the Joseph Henry House. In Washington his statue stands before the old Smithsonian Building.

LEONARDO DA VINCI

The illegitimate son of a 25-year-old notary, Ser Piero, and a peasant girl, Caterina, Leonardo was born on April 15, 1452, in Vinci, Italy, just outside Florence. His father took custody of the little fellow shortly after his birth, while his mother married someone else and moved to a neighboring town.

They kept on having kids, although not with each other, and they eventually supplied him with a total of 17 half sisters and brothers..

Growing up in his father's Vinci home, Leonardo had access to scholarly texts owned by family and friends.

He was also exposed to Vinci's longstanding painting tradition, and when he was about 15 his father apprenticed him to the renowned workshop of Andrea del Verrochio in Florence. Even as an apprentice, Leonardo demonstrated his colossal talent. Indeed, his genius seems to have seeped into a number of pieces produced by the Verrocchio's workshop from the period 1470 to 1475.

For example, one of Leonardo's first big breaks was to paint an angel in Verrochio's "Baptism of Christ," and Leonardo was so much better than his master's that Verrochio allegedly resolved never to paint again. Leonardo stayed in the Verrocchio workshop until 1477 when he set up a shingle for himself.

In search of new challenges and the big bucks, he entered the service of the Duke of Milan in 1482, abandoning his first commission in Florence, "The Adoration of the Magi".

He spent 17 years in Milan, leaving only after Duke Ludovico Sforza's fall from power in 1499. It was during these years that Leonardo hit his stride, reaching new heights of scientific and artistic achievement.

The Duke kept Leonardo busy painting and sculpting and designing elaborate court festivals, but he also put Leonardo to work designing weapons, buildings and machinery.

From 1485 to 1490, Leonardo produced a studies on loads of subjects, including nature, flying machines, geometry, mechanics, municipal construction, canals and architecture (designing everything from churches to fortresses). His studies from this period contain designs for advanced weapons, including a tank and other war vehicles, various combat devices, and submarines.

Also during this period, Leonardo produced his first anatomical studies. His Milan workshop was a veritable hive of activity, buzzing with apprentices and students.Alas, Leonardo's interests were so broad, and he was so often compelled by new subjects, that he usually failed to finish what he started.

This lack of "stick-to-it-ness" resulted in his completing only about six works in these 17 years, including "The Last Supper" and "The Virgin on the Rocks," and he left dozens of paintings and projects unfinished or unrealized (see "Big Horse" in sidebar).

He spent most of his time studying science, either by going out into nature and observing things or by locking himself away in his workshop cutting up bodies or pondering universal truths. Between 1490 and 1495 he developed his habit of recording his studies in meticulously illustrated notebooks. His work covered four main themes: painting, architecture, the elements of mechanics, and human anatomy.

These studies and sketches were collected into various codices and manuscripts, which are now hungrily collected by museums and individuals.

Back to Milan... after the invasion by the French and Ludovico Sforza's fall from power in 1499, Leonardo was left to search for a new patron.

Over the next 16 years, Leonardo worked and traveled throughout Italy for a number of employers, including the dastardly Cesare Borgia.

He traveled for a year with Borgia's army as a military engineer and even met Niccolo Machiavelli, author of "The Prince." Leonardo also designed a bridge to span the "golden horn" in Constantinople during this period and received a commission, with the help of Machiavelli, to paint the "Battle of Anghiari." About 1503, Leonardo reportedly began work on the "Mona Lisa."

On July 9, 1504, he received notice of the death of his father, Ser Piero. Through the contrivances of his meddling half brothers and sisters, Leonardo was deprived of any inheritance. The death of a beloved uncle also resulted in a scuffle over inheritance, but this time Leonardo beat out his scheming siblings and wound up with use of the uncle's land and money.

From 1513 to 1516, he worked in Rome, maintaining a workshop and undertaking a variety of projects for the Pope. He continued his studies of human anatomy and physiology, but the Pope forbade him from dissecting cadavers, which truly cramped his style.

Following the death of his patron Giuliano de' Medici in March of 1516, he was offered the title of Premier Painter and Engineer and Architect of the King by Francis I in France. His last and perhaps most generous patron, Francis I provided Leonardo with a cushy job, including a stipend and manor house near the royal chateau at Amboise.

Although suffering from a paralysis of the right hand, Leonardo was still able to draw and teach. He produced studies for the Virgin Mary from "The Virgin and Child with St. Anne", studies of cats, horses, dragons, St. George, anatomical studies, studies on the nature of water, drawings of the Deluge, and of various machines.

Leonardo died on May 2, 1519 in Cloux, France. Legend has it that King Francis was at his side when he died, cradling Leonardo's head in his arms.

MARIE CURIE

Marie Curie (born Maria Sklodowska; November 7, 1867 – July 4, 1934) was a physicist and chemist of Polish upbringing and, subsequently, French citizenship. She was a pioneer in the field of radioactivity, the first twice-honored Nobel laureate (and still the only one in two different sciences) and the first female professor at the University of Paris.

She was born in Warsaw, Congress Poland, Russian Empire, and lived there until she was 24. In 1891 she followed her elder sister to study in Paris, where she obtained her higher degrees and conducted her scientific work.

She founded the Curie Institutes in Paris and Warsaw. She was the wife of fellow-Nobel-laureate Pierre Curie and the mother of a third Nobel laureate, Irène Joliot-Curie.

While an actively loyal French citizen, she never lost her sense of Polish identity. Madame Curie named the first new chemical element that she discovered polonium for her native country.

Maria Sklodowska was born in Warsaw to Polish parents, Bronislawa and Wladyslaw Sklodowski, both of whom were teachers and instilled in their children a sense of the value of learning. Wladyslaw Sklodowski was a teacher of mathematics and physics.

Maria was the youngest of five children: Zofia (born 1862), Józef (1863), Bronislawa (1865), Helena (1866) and finally Maria (1867). Maria's early years were marked by the death of her sister Zofia (from typhus) and, two years later, the death of her mother (tuberculosis).

These events caused her to give up her Roman Catholic religion and become an agnostic. From childhood Sklodowska showed an exceptional memory and work ethic, and was known to neglect food and sleep in order to study. At age sixteen she graduated from a Russian *liceum* at the top of her class, winning a gold medal on completion of her secondary education there.

Because she was female, and because of Russian reprisals following the Polish 1863 uprising against Tsarist Russia, Sklodowska was denied admission to a regular university.

Her father having lost his savings through bad investments, Maria had to take work as a teacher while attending Warsaw's illegal Polish Floating University.

At age 18 she took a post as a governess, where she experienced an unhappy love affair. From her earnings she supported her elder sister Bronislawa, who was studying medicine in Paris, on the understanding that Bronislawa would in turn later help Maria get an education. Eventually in 1891 Maria went to join her sister in Paris.

At the University of Paris, Sklodowska studied mathematics, physics and chemistry. (Later, in 1909, she would become that University's first female professor, when she was named to her late husband's chair in physics, which he had held for only a year and a half before his tragic death.) In early 1893 she graduated first in her undergraduate class.

A year later, also at the University of Paris, she obtained her master's degree in mathematics. In 1903, under the supervision of Henri Becquerel, she received her DSc from the University of Paris, becoming the first woman in France to complete a doctorate.

At the University of Paris, also, she met and married Pierre Curie. At the time, Pierre Curie was an instructor in the School of Physics and Chemistry, the *École Supérieure de Physique et de Chimie Industrielles de la Ville de Paris* (ESPCI). Sklodowska was a student at the University of Paris, and had begun her scientific career in Paris with an investigation of the magnetic properties of various steels; it was their mutual interest in magnetism that drew Sklodowska and Curie together.

Eventually they studied radioactive materials, particularly pitchblende, the ore from which uranium was extracted. By April 1898, Sklodowska-Curie deduced that pitchblende must contain traces of an unknown substance far more radioactive than uranium.

In July 1898, Pierre and Marie together published an article announcing the existence of an element which they named polonium, in honor of her native Poland, then still partitioned among three empires. On December 26, 1898, the Curies announced the existence of a second element, which they named radium for its intense radioactivity — a word that they coined.

Over the course of several years of unceasing work in the most difficult physical conditions, they processed several tons of pitchblende, progressively concentrating the radioactive substances and eventually isolating the chloride salts (refining radium chloride on April 20, 1902).

Polonium was not yet isolated at this time. In 1903, the Royal Swedish Academy of Sciences awarded Pierre Curie, Marie Curie, and Henri Becquerel the Nobel Prize in Physics, "in recognition of the extraordinary services they have rendered by their joint researches on the radiation phenomena discovered by Professor Henri Becquerel."

Curie was the first woman to be awarded a Nobel Prize. Eight years later, she received the 1911 Nobel Prize in Chemistry, "in recognition of her services to the advancement of chemistry by the discovery of the elements radium and polonium, by the isolation of radium and the study of the nature and compounds of this remarkable element".

In an unusual decision, Sklodowska-Curie intentionally refrained from patenting the radium-isolation process so that the scientific community could do research unhindered. A month after accepting her 1911 Nobel Prize, she was hospitalized with depression and a kidney ailment. Sklodowska-Curie was the first person to win or share *two* Nobel Prizes. She is one of only two people who have been awarded a Nobel Prize in two different fields, the other being Linus Pauling (Chemistry, Peace).

She remains the only woman to have won two Nobel Prizes, and the only person to have won Nobel Prizes in two different *science* fields. Nevertheless, the French Academy of Sciences refused to abandon its prejudice against women, and she failed by one vote to be elected to membership. (Pierre had been elected to the Academy in 1905.)

On April 19, 1906, Pierre was killed in a street accident as he was leaving a publisher's office. He had gone there to review proofs of an article, and found the business closed due to a strike. Heading back across the street in heavy rain, he was struck by a horse-drawn vehicle and fell under its wheels, fracturing his skull. While it has been speculated that he may previously have been weakened by prolonged radiation exposure, it has not been proven that this was the cause of the accident. Marie was devastated by her husband's death.

She may subsequently have had an affair with physicist Paul Langevin — a married man who had left his wife — which resulted in a press scandal, exploited by her academic opponents. Despite her fame as a scientist working for France, the public's attitude to the scandal tended toward xenophobia. Langevin's grandson Michel Langevin later married Sklodowska-Curie's granddaughter,

Hélène Joliot. During World War I, Sklodowska-Curie pushed for the use of mobile radiography units, which came to be popularly known as *petites Curies* ("Little Curies"), for the treatment of wounded soldiers. These units were powered using tubes of *radium emanation*, a colorless, radioactive gas given off by radium, later identified as radon.

Sklodowska-Curie personally provided the tubes, derived from the radium she purified. Also, promptly after the war started, she donated her and her husband's gold Nobel Prize medals for the war effort.

After World War I, in 1921 and again in 1929, Sklodowska-Curie toured the United States, where she was welcomed triumphantly, to raise funds for research on radium. These distractions from her scientific labors, and the attendant publicity, caused her much discomfort but provided resources for her work.

Her second American tour succeeded in equipping the Warsaw Radium Institute, founded in 1925, with her sister Bronislawa as director.

In her later years, Sklodowska-Curie headed the Pasteur Institute and a radioactivity laboratory created for her by the University of Paris. Her death near Sallanches, Savoy, in 1934 was from aplastic anemia, almost certainly due to exposure to radiation, as the damaging effects of ionising radiation were not yet known, and much of her work had been carried out in a shed with no safety measures.

She had carried test tubes containing radioactive isotopes in her pocket and stored them in her desk drawer, remarking on the pretty blue-green light the substances gave off in the dark.

She was interred at the cemetery in Sceaux, where Pierre lay, but sixty years later, in 1995, in honor of their work, the remains of both were transferred to the Panthéon in Paris. The Curies' elder daughter, Irène Joliot-Curie, won a Nobel Prize for Chemistry in 1935 for discovering that aluminium could be radioactive and emit neutrons when bombarded with alpha rays.

The younger daughter, Ève Curie, wrote the biography, *Madame Curie*, after her mother's death. As one of the most famous female scientists to date, Marie Curie has been an icon in the scientific world and has inspired many tributes and recognitions.

In 1995, she was the first and only woman laid to rest under the famous dome of the Panthéon, in Paris, on her own merits, alongside her husband. The curie (symbol Ci), a unit of radioactivity, is named in their honour, as is the element with atomic number 96 - curium.

Sklodowska-Curie's likeness appeared on the Polish late-1980s inflationary 20,000-zloty banknote. Her likeness also appeared on stamps and coins, and on the last French 500-franc note, with her husband, before the franc was made obsolete by the euro.

Three radioactive minerals are named after the Curies: curite, sklodowskite, and cupros klodows kite. Pierre and Marie Curie University, the largest science, technology and medicine university in France, and successor institution to the faculty of science at the University of Paris, where she taught, is named in honour of her and Pierre. The university is home to the laboratory where they discovered radium.

Another school named for her, Marie Curie M.S. 158, in Bayside, New York, specializes in science and technology as does Curie Metropolitan High School, located in the community area of Archer Heights on Chicago's Southwest Side. It has a Technical, Performing Arts and IB program.

In 2007, the Pierre Curie Paris Métro station was renamed the "Pierre et Marie Curie" station. The Maria Sklodowska-Curie Medallion, a stained-glass panel created by Jozef C. Mazur, may be found at the University at Buffalo Polish Room. A KLM McDonnell Douglas MD-11 (registration PH-KCC) is named in her honor.

MICHAEL FARADAY

Faraday's parents were members of the obscure religious denomination of the Sandemanians, and Faraday himself, shortly after his marriage, at the age of thirty, joined the same sect, to which he adhered till his death. Religion and science he kept strictly apart, believing that the data of science were of an entirely different nature from the direct communications between God and the soul on which his religious faith was based.

The son of a blacksmith who became one of the greatest scientists of the 19th century. His work on electricity and magnetism not only revolutionized physics, but has led to so much in our lifestyles today which depend on them (including computers and telephone lines and so Web sites).

Faraday was a devoutly Christian member of the Sandemanians, which significantly influenced upon him and strongly affected the way in which he approached and interpreted nature. The Sandemanians originated from Presbyterians who had rejected the idea of state churches, and tried to go back to a New Testament type of Christianity.

Farday's work propelled him into the limelight. By 1826 he was head of the Royal Institution, founded... to provide scientific education for the masses. Offered the presidency of the Royal Society, Faraday flatly refused, as he also refused the offer of a knighthood. He did not believe Christ of the apostles would accept these worldly honors...

Farada's scientific achievements, among the greatest in history, sprang from his religious faith. As a lifelong member of a sect called the Sandemanians, he believed that nature substantiates the existence of its Creator.

Because one God created the world, all of nature mut be interconnected as a single whole, he believed. Therefore, electricity and magnetism must be interlinked. This view of nature was the very view emphasized by the Sandemanians. Key to Faraday's thought was the idea that objective reality must judge every theory, no matter how elegant and sophisticated...

Michael served as a lay preacher in the Sandemanians throughout his life. Sandemanians, an offshoot of the Scottish Presbyterian Church, believed in practicing primitive Christianity (that is, Christianity as the apostles practiced it).

They urged separation of church and state. They observed communion in conjunction with footwashing and love feasts. They were so strict that when Faraday appeared before Queen Victoria at her request, he was temporarily excommunicated because his attendance had been required at church.

His faith gave him the courage to turn down a government request that he develop poison gases for use in the Crimean War. He refused to buy insurance, believing that to do so was to show lack of faith... Although he was happily married to Sarah Bernard, a fellow Sandemanian, the Faradays had no children. When he died, he was buried, at his own request, beneath a simple headstone.

His successor, the physicist John Tyndall, called Michael Faraday, "the greatest experimental philosopher the world has ever known."

Faraday's family were Sandemanians, followers of the 18th century deposed Scottish Presbyterian minister John Glas and of his minister son-in-law Robert Sandeman, who died in Danbury, CT, after seven years sojourn in colonial America (he established six churches here).

Faraday himself did not join the church until one month after his marriage to Sarah Barnard (he was 30, she 21); he became an elder and had to preach occasionally (a book of four of his sermons was printed; a Sandeman lent me a copy when I was at Oxford. At that time I visited a surviving church in Edinburgh and had dinner with the clerk of the one in London).

The Sandemanians are opposed to any established church; they believe strictly in the Bible and in Christ. In a London sermon Faraday himself said, "I cannot do better than to read to you the words of the Scripture instead of multiplying my own words."

In a letter (1844) to Lady Lovelace, he noted, "In my intercourse with my fellow creatures that which is religious and that which is philosophical have ever been distinct things." The agnostic Tyndall commented unsympathetically, "When Faraday opened the door of the oratory, he closed that of the laboratory." Consequently he has often been held up as the example par excellence of the compartmentalization of science and religion.

Closer examination, however, reveals that his attitudes towards both are quite similar. They are both rooted in the same experimental view of nature. In his only public address involving science and religion (Prince Consort Albert in the audience) he confessed, "The book of nature which we have to read is written by the finger of God."

This lecture is published at the end of a volume on Experimental Researches in Chemistry and Physics, where he states, "These observations are so immediately connected in their nature and origin with my own experimental life; either as a cause or a

NICOLAS COPERNICUS

Copernicus (1473-1543) is said to be the founder of modern astronomy. He was born in Poland, and eventually was sent off to Cracow University, there to study mathematics and optics; at Bologna, canon law.

Returning from his studies in Italy, Copernicus, through the influence of his uncle, was appointed as a canon in the cathedral of Frauenburg where he spent a sheltered and academic life for the rest of his days. Because of his clerical position, Copernicus moved in the highest circles of power; but a student he remained. For relaxation Copernicus painted and translated Greek poetry into Latin. His interest in astronomy gradually grew to be one in which he had a primary interest. His investigations were carried on quietly and alone, without help or consultation.

He made his celestial observations from a turret situated on the protective wall around the cathedral, observations were made "bare eyeball," so to speak, as a hundred more years were to pass consequence, that I have thought the close of this volun unfit place for their reproduction."

He believed the universe is intelligible, beautiful, and ac to man's usedesigned by a rational, wise, and good God. H "The beauty of electricity, or of any other force, is not t power is mysterious and unexpected, but that it is under la that the taught intellect can even now govern it." And so, he s relations among the various forces in a unified nature: ele magnetic, and even gravitational.

He regarded facts as fundamental, the observed ones of sci and the revealed ones of religion. Each group, howeve surrounded by an aura of speculation, i.e., theory or theolog

If these auras are large, overlap will occur and inevitable confl owing to the incompleteness and imperfection of each. (Everyo I believe, will continually experience such personal conflicts science and religion, but hopefully they will change as one matures In Faraday's case speculation was relatively less important so tha the apparently independent facts remained separated-withou conflict.

Faraday's life was consistent with his faith and hope. He had an unquenchable thirst for truth, but he recognized his own limitations. He pursued truth industriously throughout his whole life. Above all, he had great humility, born out of reverence for God and His universe, man and his environment.

Tyndall noted that in Faraday's case, "You cannot separate the moral and the emotional from the intellectual." This irreligious colleague described him in Christian terms, "blameless, of good behavior, apt to teach, not greedy of filthy lucre, but patient".

before the invention of the telescope. In 1530, Copernicus completed and gave to the world his great work *De Revolutionibus*, which asserted that the earth rotated on its axis once daily and traveled around the sun once yearly: a fantastic concept for the times.

Up to the time of Copernicus the thinkers of the western world believed in the Ptolemiac theory that the universe was a closed space bounded by a spherical envelope beyond which there was nothing. Claudius Ptolemy, an Egyptian living in Alexandria, at about 150 A.D., gathered and organized the thoughts of the earlier thinkers. (It is to be noted that one of the ancient Greek astronomers, Aristarchus, did have ideas similar to those more fully developed by Copernicus but they were rejected in favour of the geocentric or earth-centered scheme as was espoused by Aristotle.)

Ptolemy's findings were that the earth was a fixed, inert, immovable mass, located at the center of the universe, and all celestial bodies, including the sun and the fixed stars, revolved around it. It was a theory that appealed to human nature. It fit with the casual observations that a person might want to make in the field; and second, it fed man's ego.

Copernicus was in no hurry to publish his theory, though parts of his work were circulated among a few of the astronomers that were giving the matter some thought; indeed, Copernicus' work might not have ever reached the printing press if it had not been for a young man who sought out the master in 1539.

George Rheticus was a 25 year old German mathematics professor who was attracted to the 66 year old cleric, having read one of his papers. Intending to spend a few weeks with Copernicus, Rheticus ended up staying as a house guest for two years, so fascinated was he with Copernicus and his theories.

Now, up to this time, Copernicus was reluctant to publish, — not so much that he was concerned with what the church might say about his novel theory (*De Revolutionibus* was placed on the Index in 1616 and only removed in 1835), but rather because he was a perfectionist and he never thought, even after working on it for thirty years, that his complete work was ready, — there were, as far as Copernicus was concerned, observations to be checked and rechecked.

(Interestingly, Copernicus' original manuscript, lost to the world for 300 years, was located in Prague in the middle of the 19th century; it shows Copernicus' pen was, it would appear, continually in motion with revision after revision; all in Latin as was the vogue for scholarly writings in those days.)

Copernicus died in 1543 and was never to know what a stir his work had caused. It went against the philosophical and religious beliefs that had been held during the medieval times. Man, it was believed (and still believed by some) was made by God in His image, man was the next thing to God, and, as such, superior, especially in his best part, his soul, to all creatures, indeed this part was not even part of the natural world (a philosophy which has proved disastrous to the earth's environment as any casual observer of the 20th century might confirm by simply looking about).

Copernicus' theories might well lead men to think that they are simply part of nature and not superior to it and that ran counter to the theories of the politically powerful churchmen of the time.

Two other Italian scientists of the time, Galileo and Bruno, embraced the Copernican theory unreservedly and as a result suffered much personal injury at the hands of the powerful church inquisitors.

Giordano Bruno had the audacity to even go beyond Copernicus, and, dared to suggest, that space was boundless and that the sun was and its planets were but one of any number of similar systems: Why! — there even might be other inhabited worlds with rational beings equal or possibly superior to ourselves.

For such blasphemy, Bruno was tried before the Inquisition, condemned and burned at the stake in 1600. Galileo was brought forward in 1633, and, there, in front of his "betters," he was, under the threat of torture and death, forced to his knees to renounce all belief in Copernican theories, and was thereafter sentenced to imprisonment for the remainder of his days.

The most important aspect of Copernicus' work is that it forever changed the place of man in the cosmos; no longer could man legitimately think his significance greater than his fellow creatures; with Copernicus' work, man could now take his place among that which exists all about him, and not of necessity take that premier position which had been assigned immodestly to him by the theologians.

"Of all discoveries and opinions, none may have exerted a greater effect on the human spirit than the doctrine of Copernicus. The world had scarcely become known as round and complete in itself when it was asked to waive the tremendous privilege of being the center of the universe. Never, perhaps, was a greater demand made on mankind - for by this admission so many things vanished in mist and smoke!

What became of our Eden, our world of innocence, piety and poetry; the testimony of the senses; the conviction of a poetic - religious faith? No wonder his contemporaries did not wish to let all this go and offered every possible resistance to a doctrine which in its converts authorized and demanded a freedom of view and greatness of thought so far unknown, indeed not even dreamed of."

NIELS BOHR

Niels Henrik David Bohr was born in Copenhagen in 1885 to Christian Bohr, a professor of physiology at the University of Copenhagen and a Nobel Prize winner, and Ellen Adler Bohr, who came from a wealthy Sephardic Jewish family prominent in Danish banking and parliamentary circles.

Bohr received his doctorate from Copenhagen University in 1911 and then studied under Ernest Rutherford in the Victoria University in Manchester, England.

In 1911, Bohr visited Cambridge, where he followed the experimental work occurring in the Cavendish Laboratory under Sir J.J. Thomson's guidance and pursued his own theoretical studies.

In 1912, he worked in Professor Rutherford's laboratory in Manchester. Based on Rutherford's theories, Bohr published his model of atomic structure in 1913, which is still commonly used and taught today as an educational simplification.

The model introduced the theory of electrons traveling in orbits around the atom's nucleus, the chemical properties of the element being largely determined by the number of electrons in the outer orbits.

Bohr also introduced the idea that an electron could drop from a higher-energy orbit to a lower one, emitting a photon (light quantum) of discrete energy. This became the basis for quantum theory.

Following in his father's footsteps, in 1916, Bohr became a professor at the University of Copenhagen. In 1920, he became director of the newly constructed "Institute of Theoretical Physics" and was awarded the Nobel Prize in Physics in 1922 "for his services in the investigation of the structure of atoms and of the radiation emanating from them."

After 1930, Bohr's activities in his Institute were focused on research on the constitution of the atomic nuclei and of their transmutations and disintegrations. He also contributed to the clarification of the problems encountered in quantum physics, which is discussed in several essays written between 1933 and 1962.

In 1943, shortly before he was to be arrested by the German police, Bohr escaped to Sweden and then traveled to London. He worked at Los Alamos on the Manhattan Project, where he was allegedly known by the assumed name of Nicholas Baker for security reasons.

However, his role in the project was minor, as he was seen as a knowledgeable consultant. After the war, he returned to Copenhagen, advocating for a peaceful use of nuclear energy. In 1955 he organized the first Atoms for Peace Conference in Geneva, Switzerland.

Bohr and his wife Margrethe had six children, one of whom, Aage Niels Bohr, became a very successful physicist and also won a Nobel Prize. Bohr died in Copenhagen in 1962. The element bohrium is named in his honor.

NIKOLA TESLA

Nikola Tesla symbolizes a unifying force and inspiration for all nations in the name of peace and science. He was a true visionary far ahead of his contemporaries in the field of scientific development. New York State and many other states in the USA proclaimed July 10, Tesla's birthday- Nikola Tesla Day.

Many United States Congressmen gave speeches in the House of Representatives on July 10, 1990 celebrating the 134th anniversary of scientist-inventor Nikola Tesla. Senator Levine from Michigan spoke in the US Senate on the same occasion.

The street sign "Nikola Tesla Corner" was recently placed on the corner of the 40th Street and 6th Avenue in Manhattan. There is a large photo of Tesla in the Statue of Liberty Museum. The Liberty Science Center in Jersey City, New Jersey has a daily science demonstration of the Tesla Coil creating a million volts of electricity before the spectators eyes.

Many books were written about Tesla : Prodigal Genius: The Life of Nikola Tesla by John J. O'Neill and Margaret Cheney's book Tesla: Man out of Time has contributed significantly to his fame. A documentary film Nikola Tesla, The Genius Who Lit the World, produced by the Tesla Memorial Society and the Nikola Tesla Museum in Belgrade, The Secret of Nikola Tesla (Orson Welles), BBC Film Masters of the Ionosphere are other tributes to the great genius.

Nikola Tesla was born on July 10, 1856 in Smiljan, Lika, which was then part of the Austo-Hungarian Empire, region of Croatia. His father, Milutin Tesla was a Serbian Orthodox Priest and his mother Djuka Mandič was an inventor in her own right of household appliances.

Tesla studied at the Realschule, Karlstadt in 1873, the Polytechnic Institute in Graz, Austria and the University of Prague. At first, he intended to specialize in physics and mathematics, but soon he became fascinated with electricity. He began his career as an electrical engineer with a telephone company in Budapest in 1881.

It was there, as Tesla was walking with a friend through the city park that the elusive solution to the rotating magnetic field flashed through his mind. With a stick, he drew a diagram in the sand explaining to his friend the principle of the induction motor. Before going to America, Tesla joined Continental Edison Company in Paris where he designed dynamos.

While in Strassbourg in 1883, he privately built a prototype of the induction motor and ran it successfully. Unable to interest anyone in Europe in promoting this radical device, Tesla accepted an offer to work for Thomas Edison in New York. His childhood dream was to come to America to harness the power of Niagara Falls.

Young Nikola Tesla came to the United States in 1884 with an introduction letter from Charles Batchelor to Thomas Edison: "I know two great men," wrote Batchelor, "one is you and the other is this young man." Tesla spent the next 59 years of his productive life living in New York. Tesla set about improving Edison's line of dynamos while working in Edison's lab in New Jersey. It was here that his divergence of opinion with Edison over direct current versus alternating current began. This disagreement climaxed in the war of the currents as Edison fought a losing battle to protect his investment in direct current equipment and facilities.

Tesla pointed out the inefficiency of Edison's direct current electrical powerhouses that have been build up and down the Atlantic seaboard. The secret, he felt, lay in the use of alternating current ,because to him all energies were cyclic. Why not build generators that would send electrical energy along distribution lines first one way, than another, in multiple waves using the polyphase principle?

Edison's lamps were weak and inefficient when supplied by direct current. This system had a severe disadvantage in that it could not be transported more than two miles due to its inability to step up to high voltage levels necessary for long distance transmission. Consequently, a direct current power station was required at two mile intervals.

Direct current flows continuously in one direction; alternating current changes direction 50 or 60 times per second and can be stepped up to vary high voltage levels, minimizing power loss across great distances. The future belongs to alternating current.

Nikola Tesla developed polyphase alternating current system of generators, motors and transformers and held 40 basic U.S. patents on the system, which George Westinghouse bought, determined to supply America with the Tesla system. Edison did not want to lose his DC empire, and a bitter war ensued. This was the war of the currents between AC and DC. Tesla -Westinghouse ultimately emerged the victor because AC was a superior technology. It was a war won for the progress of both America and the world.

Tesla introduced his motors and electrical systems in a classic paper, "A New System of Alternating Current Motors and Transformers" which he delivered before the American Institute of Electrical Engineers in 1888. One of the most impressed was the industrialist and inventor George Westinghouse. One day he visited Tesla's laboratory and was amazed at what he saw.

Tesla had constructed a model polyphase system consisting of an alternating current dynamo, step-up and step-down transformers and A.C. motor at the other end. The perfect partnership between Tesla and Westinghouse for the nationwide use of electricity in America had begun.

In February 1882, Tesla discovered the rotating magnetic field, a fundamental principle in physics and the basis of nearly all devices that use alternating current. Tesla brilliantly adapted the principle of rotating magnetic field for the construction of alternating current induction motor and the polyphase system for the generation, transmission, distribution and use of electrical power.

Tesla's A.C. induction motor is widely used throughout the world in industry and household appliances. It started the industrial revolution at the turn of the century. Electricity today is generated transmitted and converted to mechanical power by means of his inventions. Tesla's greatest achievement is his polyphase alternating current system, which is today lighting the entire globe.

Tesla astonished the world by demonstrating. the wonders of alternating current electricity at the World Columbian Exposition in Chicago in 1893. Alternating current became standard power in the 20th Century. This accomplishment changed the world. He designed the first hydroelectric powerplant in Niagara Falls in 1895, which was the final victory of alternating current.

The achievement was covered widely in the world press, and Tesla was praised as a hero world wide. King Nikola of Montenegro conferred upon him the Order of Danilo.

Tesla was a pioneer in many fields. The Tesla coil, which he invented in 1891, is widely used today in radio and television sets and other electronic equipment. That year also marked the date of Tesla's United States citizenship.

His alternating current induction motor is considered one of the ten greatest discoveries of all time. Among his discoveries are the fluorescent light, laser beam, wireless communications, wireless transmission of electrical energy, remote control, robotics, Tesla's turbines and vertical take off aircraft. Tesla is the father of the radio and the modern electrical transmissions systems.

He registered over 700 patents worldwide. His vision included exploration of solar energy and the power of the sea. He foresaw interplanetary communications and satellites.

The Century Magazine published Tesla's principles of telegraphy without wires, popularizing scientific lectures given before Franklin Institute in February 1893.

The Electrical Review in 1896 published X-rays of a man, made by Tesla, with X-ray tubes of his own design. They appeared at the same time as when Roentgen announced his discovery of X-rays.

Tesla never attempted to proclaim priority. Roentgen congratulated Tesla on his sophisticated X-ray pictures, and Tesla even wrote Roentgen's name on one of his films.

He experimented with shadowgraphs similar to those that later were to be used by Wilhelm Rontgen when he discovered X-rays in 1895. Tesla's countless experiments included work on a carbon button lamp, on the power of electrical resonance, and on various types of lightning. Tesla invented the special vacuum tube which emitted light to be used in photography.

The breadth of his inventions is demonstrated by his patents for a bladeless steam turbine based on a spiral flow principle. Tesla also patented a pump design to operate at extremely high temperature.

Nikola Tesla patented the basic system of radio in 1896. His published schematic diagrams describing all the basic elements of the radio transmitter which was later used by Marconi. In 1896 Tesla constructed an instrument to receive radio waves.

He experimented with this device and transmitted radio waves from his laboratory on South 5th Avenue. to the Gerlach Hotel at

27th Street in Manhattan. The device had a magnet which gave off intense magnetic fields up to 20,000 lines per centimeter. The radio device clearly establishes his piority in the discovery of radio.

The shipboard quench-spark transmitter produced by the Lowenstein Radio Company and licensed under Nikola Tesla Company patents, was installed on the U.S. Naval vessels prior to World War I.

In December 1901, Marconi established wireless communication between Britain and the United States earning him the Nobel prize in 1909. But much of Marconi's work was not original. In 1864, James Maxwell theorized electromagnetic waves.

In 1887, Heinrich Hertz proved Maxwell's theories. Later, Sir Oliver Logde extended the Hertz prototype system. The Brandley coherer increased the distance messages could be transmitted. The coherer was perfected by Marconi.

However, the heart of radio transmission is based upon four tuned circuits for transmitting and receiving. It is Tesla's original concept demonstrated in his famous lecture at the Franklin Institute in Philadelphia in 1893. The four circuits, used in two pairs, are still a fundamental part of all radio and television equipment.

The United States Supreme Court, in 1943 held Marconi's most important patent invalid, recognizing Tesla's more significant contribution as the inventor of radio technology. Tesla built an experimental station in Colorado Springs, Colorado in 1899, to experiment with high voltage, high frequency electricity and other phenomena.

When the Colorado Springs Tesla Coil magnifying transmitter was energized, it created sparks 30 feet long. From the outside antenna, these sparks could be seen from a distance of ten miles. From this laboratory, Tesla generated and sent out wireless waves which mediated energy, without wires for miles.

In Colorado Springs, where he stayed from May 1899 until 1900, Tesla made what he regarded as his most important discovery—terrestrial stationary waves. By this discovery he proved that the

Earth could be used as a conductor and would be as responsive as a tuning fork to electrical vibrations of a certain frequency. He also lighted 200 lamps without wires from a distance of 25 miles(40 kilometers) and created man-made lightning. At one time he was certain he had received signals from another planet in his Colorado laboratory, a claim that was met with disbelief in some scientific journals.

The old Waldorf Astoria was the residence of Nikola Tesla for many years. He lived there when he was at the height of financial and intellectual power. Tesla organized elaborate dinners, inviting famous people who later witnessed spectacular electrical experiments in his laboratory. Financially supported by J. Pierpont Morgan, Tesla built the Wardenclyffe laboratory and its famous transmitting tower in Shoreham, Long Island between 1901 and 1905.

This huge landmark was 187 feet high, capped by a 68-foot copper dome which housed the magnifying transmitter. It was planned to be the first broadcast system, transmitting both signals and power without wires to any point on the globe. The huge magnifying transmitter, discharging high frequency electricity, would turn the earth into a gigantic dynamo which would project its electricity in unlimited amounts anywhere in the world.

Tesla's concept of wireless electricity was used to power ocean liners, destroy warships, run industry and transportation and send communications instantaneously all over the globe. To stimulate the public's imagination, Tesla suggested that this wireless power could even be used for interplanetary communication. If Tesla were confident to reach Mars, how much less difficult to reach Paris. Many newspapers and periodicals interviewed Tesla and described his new system for supplying wireless power to run all of the earth's industry.

Because of a dispute between Morgan and Tesla as to the final use of the tower. Morgan withdrew his funds. The financier's classic comment was, "If anyone can draw on the power, where do we put the meter?"

The erected, but incomplete tower was demolished in 1917 for wartime security reasons. The site where the Wardenclyffe tower stood still exists with its 100 feet deep foundation still intact. Tesla's laboratory designed by Stanford White in 1901 is today still in good condition and is graced with a bicentennial plaque. Tesla lectured to the scientific community on his inventions in New York, Philadelphia and St. Louis and before scientific organizations in both England and France in 1892.

Tesla's lectures and writings of the 1890s aroused wide admiration among contemporaries popularized his inventions and inspired untold numbers of younger men to enter the new field of radio and electrical science.

Nikola Tesla was one of the most celebrated personalities in the American press, in this century. According to Life Magazine's special issue of September, 1997, Tesla is among the 100 most famous people of the last 1,000 years. He is one of the great men who divert the stream of human history. Tesla's celebrity was in its height at the turn of the century. His discoveries, inventions and vision had widespread acceptance by the public, the scientific community and American press.

Tesla's discoveries had extensive coverage in the scientific journals, the daily and weekly press as well as in the foremost literary and intellectual publications of the day. He was the Super Star. Tesla wrote many autobiographical articles for the prominent journal Electrical Experimenter, collected in the book, My Inventions.

Tesla was gifted with intense powers of visualization and exceptional memory from early youth on. He was able to fully construct, develop and perfect his inventions completely in his mind before committing them to paper.

According to Hugo Gernsback, Tesla was possessed of a striking physical appearance over six feet tall with deep set eyes and a stately manner. His impressions of Tesla, were of a man endowed with remarkable physical and mental freshness, ready to surprise the world with more and more inventions as he grew older.

A lifelong bachelor he led a somewhat isolated existence, devoting his full energies to science. In 1894, he was given honorary doctoral degrees by Columbia and Yale University and the Elliot Cresson medal by the Franklin Institute.

In 1934, the city of Philadelphia awarded him the John Scott medal for his polyphase power system. He was an honorary member of the National Electric Light Association and a fellow of the American Association for the Advancement of Science.

On one occasion, he turned down an invitation from Kaiser Wilhelm II to come to Germany to demonstrate his experiments and to receive a high decoration.

In 1915, a New York Times article announced that Tesla and Edison were to share the Nobel Prize for physics. Oddly, neither man received the prize, the reason being unclear. It was rumored that Tesla refused the prize because he would not share with Edison, and because Marconi had already received his. Tesla died on January 7th, 1943 in the Hotel New Yorker, where he had lived for the last ten years of his life.

ROBERT BOYLE

Robert Boyle was born on 25 Jan 1627 in Lismore, County Waterford, Ireland. Robert Boyle was born into a Protestant family. His father was Richard Boyle, Earl of Cork, who had left England in 1588 at the age of 22 and gone to Ireland. Appointed clerk of the council of Munster by Elizabeth I in 1600, he bought Sir Walter Raleigh's estates in the counties of Cork, Waterford, and Tipperary two years later. Robert's mother, Catherine Fenton, was Richard Boyle's second wife, his first having died within a year of the birth of their first child.

Robert was the seventh son (and fourteenth child) of his parents fifteen children (twelve of the fifteen survived childhood). Richard Boyle was in his 60s and Catherine Boyle in her 40s when Robert was born. Of his father Robert would later write:-

He, by God's blessing on his prosperous industry, from very inconsiderable beginnings, built so plentiful and so eminent a fortune, that his prosperity has found many admirers, but few parallels. Indeed, Robert was fortunate to have the richest man in Great Britain for a father although, one would have to say, the Earl of Cork had acquired his fortune by somewhat dubious means. He was imprisoned in England on charges of embezzlement at one stage and later was fined heavily for possessing defective titles to some of his estates.

The Earl of Cork and his wife believed that the best upbringing for young children, up to the time they began their education, could be provided away from their parents. Robert was sent away to be brought up in the country while his father continued to aim for higher and higher political success.

The Earl of Cork lived for four years in his town house in Dublin. He was appointed a lord high justice in 1629 and lord high treasurer in 1631. However, during this time in Dublin Robert's mother died and some time after this Robert returned from his stay with his country nurse to rejoin his family.

Robert was sent, together with one of his brothers, to study at Eton College in England in 1635. At this time the school was becoming fashionable as a place where important people sent their sons. The headmaster was John Harrison and the two young Boyle brothers lived in the headmaster's house:-

Besides the strictly classical course of study then in vogue, the boys had private tutors in French, dancing, and music, for whom they paid extra fees.

Boyle paid tribute to Harrison in where he writes that Harrison gave him a:- ... *strong passion to acquire knowledge* ...

At this stage of his time at Eton, Boyle's education was clearly going well. He was popular with both his headmaster and his fellow pupils. However, perhaps he had been given too much special attention by Harrison for, when Harrison retired, Boyle seemed unable to fit in with the educational discipline the new headmaster brought to the school.

Realising that neither of his sons were progressing well at school under the new headmaster, the Earl of Cork took his sons away from the Eton in November 1638. After this Boyle was tutored privately by one of his father's chaplains.

At the age of 12 Boyle was sent by his father, with one of his brothers, on a European tour. From Dieppe they travelled to Paris, then on to Lyon before reaching Geneva. In Geneva Boyle studied with a private tutor French, Latin, rhetoric and religion. He also spent time in the afternoons playing tennis and fencing. Perhaps most importantly of all he began to study mathematics and soon:-

... he grew very well acquainted with the most useful part of arithmetic, geometry, with its subordinates, the doctrine of the sphere, that of the globe, and fortification.

In 1641 Boyle learnt Italian in preparation for visiting there. In September of that year Boyle and his tutor were in Venice, then by the beginning of 1642 they were in Florence. Galileo died in his villa in Arcetri, near Florence, while Boyle was living in the city. He was much influenced by this event and he carefully studied Galileo's works. If any one event shaped Boyle's life and directed him towards science, then it was this.

Of course his Protestant background, with an ingrained fear of Jesuits, contributed to his sympathy for Galileo and his treatment by the Roman Catholic Church. Boyle became a strong supporter of Galileo's philosophy and believed strongly from this time in the new approach to studying the world through mathematics and mechanics.

By May 1642 Boyle and his tutor were in Marseilles waiting for money from Boyle's father so that he could complete the journey home. This did not arrive, merely a letter from his father explaining that a rebellion in Munster was fully occupying his time and money. He did send pond 250 to pay for Boyle's return, but the money never reached him.

Boyle returned to Geneva where he seems to have lived mainly on his tutor's earnings, while his father continued to fight the Irish at Lismore Castle. King Charles I negotiated a cease-fire with the Catholic rebels fighting the Earl of Cork so that he might bring his troops back to England to help him in the civil war which had broken out. The Earl of Cork never got over Charles treating the

Irish as equals and he died shortly after in September 1643. Robert Boyle was still living in Geneva when his father died. In the summer of 1644 he sold some jewellery and used the money that he was paid to finance his return trip to England.

Back in England, Boyle lived for a while with his sister Katherine. She was thirteen years older than him and was a lady of some importance, married to Viscount Ranelagh. England was in a chaotic state, the civil war which had began in 1642 was being fought between King Charles and the parliament.

Charles had moved to Oxford while the parliament had formed a treaty with the Scots. In return for Scots military support they were promised the establishment of a Presbyterian church. Several battles in 1644 left both King and parliament somewhat in disarray. Boyle had property in England, the manor of Stalbridge, left to him by his father but the situation in the country made things difficult. He wrote in a letter:-

I got safe into England towards the middle of the year 1644, *where we found things in such a confusion, that although the manor of Stalbridge were by my father's decease descended unto me, yet it was near four months before I could get thither.*

In fact although Boyle inspected his new home after four months, it was much longer before he was able to move in. This happened in March 1646 after he had spent more time with his sister and made a return trip to France to repay his debts to his tutor who continued to live there. Although Boyle did not intend to spend long at Stalbridge, he remained there for around six years. He probably studied harder than he admits in a letter sent to his old tutor in France in October 1646:-

As for my studies, I have had the opportunity to prosecute them but by fits and snatches, as my leisure and my occasions would give me leave. Divers little essays, both in verse and prose, I have taken pains to scribble upon several subjects. ... The other humane studies I apply myself to, are natural philosophy, the mechanics and husbandry, according to the principles of our new philosophical college ...

This "new philosophical college" is also called by Boyle the "Invisible College" later in the letter. It is the society which would soon became the "Royal Society of London" and it provided Boyle's only contact with the world of science while he lived a somewhat lonely life at Stalbridge. He would look forward to his visits to London where members of the College:- .. *do now and then honour me with their company.*

It was discussions in the Invisible College which led to Boyle reading Oughtred's *Clavis Mathematica* as well as the works of Mersenne and Gassendi. Boyle had from the time of his visit to Italy favoured the ideas of Copernicus and he now held these views deeply, together with a deep belief in the atomic theory of matter. In the Invisible College these views were considered to be those of the new natural philosophy.

This period was a difficult one for Boyle for he tried hard not to be forced to take sides in the civil war. His loyalties were somewhat divided, his father having been a staunch Royalist, his sister Katherine a staunch Parliamentarian. Basically he had little sympathy with either side, but the final outcome of the civil war turned out to his advantage. Charles I was defeated and executed but, in 1650, Charles II landed in Scotland and tried to regain power. Cromwell, leading the parliamentary forces, defeated the Scots in 1650, again in 1651, and the Irish were also defeated by Cromwell in 1652.

Boyle went to Ireland in 1652 to look after his estates there. He ended up a very rich man when Cromwell apportioned Irish lands to the English colonists. From that time on he was able to devote himself entirely to science without the need to earn money. It should be noted, however, that Boyle was a very generous man with his money, and many around him benefited from this generosity.

Boyle met John Wilkins, the leader of the Invisible College, in London when he visited there in 1653. At this time Wilkins had just been appointed as Warden of Wadham College in Oxford and he was planning to run the Invisible College from there. He strongly encouraged Boyle to join them in Oxford and invited him to live in the College. Boyle decided to go to Oxford but preferred not to accept Wilkins' offer of accommodation, choosing instead to arrange his own rooms where he could carry out his scientific experiments.

At Oxford he joined a group of forward looking scientists, including John Wilkins, John Wallis who was the Savilian Professor of Geometry, Seth Ward who was the Savilian Professor of Astronomy, and Christopher Wren who would succeed Ward as Savilian Professor of Astronomy in 1661. From 1654 Boyle lived in Oxford, although he never held any university post.

He made important contributions to physics and chemistry and is best known for Boyle's law (sometimes called Mariotte's Law) describing an ideal gas. Boyle's law appears in an appendix written in 1662 to his work *New Experiments Physio-Mechanicall, Touching the Spring of the Air and its Effects* (1660). The 1660 text was the result of three years of experimenting with an air pump with the help of Hooke who he employed as his assistant.

The apparatus had been designed by Hooke and using it Boyle had discovered a whole series of important facts. He had shown, among other things, that sound did not travel in a vacuum, he had proved that flame required air as did life, and he investigated the elastic properties of air.

The 1662 appendix did not only contain Boyle's law which relates volume and pressure in a gas, but it also contained a defence of Boyle's work on the vacuum which appeared in the main text. Many scientists, particularly Hobbes, had argued that a vacuum could not exist and claimed that Boyle's results obtained with the vacuum pump must be the result of some as yet undiscovered force. Another book by Boyle in 1666 was called *Hydrostatic paradoxes*. It is:-

... both a penetrating critique of Pascal's work on hydrostatics, full of acute observations upon Pascal's experimental method, and a presentation of a series of important and ingenious experiments on fluid pressure.

In *The Sceptical Chemist* (1661) Boyle argued against Aristotle's view of the four elements of earth, air, fire and water. He argued that matter was composed of corpuscles which themselves were differently built up of different configurations of primary particles. Although many ideas in this work were taken over from Descartes, in one respect he fundamentally disagreed with him. Boyle's ideas that the primary particles move freely in fluids, less freely in solids, followed Descartes.

However, Descartes did not believe in a vacuum, rather he believed in an all pervading ether. Boyle had conducted many experiments which led him to believe in a vacuum and, having found no experimental evidence of the ether, to reject that idea. He did follow Descartes in his overall belief that the world was basically a complex system governed by a small number of simple mathematical laws. In considering optics, in particular colour, Boyle was not so successful.

He published *Experiments and considerations touching colours* in 1664 but was quite prepared to acknowledge that Hooke's work of 1665 was superior and he completely acknowledged that Newton's ideas, published in 1672, should replace his own.

Boyle was a founding fellow of the Royal Society. He published his results on the physical properties of air through this Society. His work in chemistry was aimed at establishing it as a mathematical science based on a mechanistic theory of matter. It is for this reason that we have decided to include Boyle into this archive of mathematicians for, although he did not develop any mathematical ideas himself, he was one of the first to argue that all science should be developed as an application of mathematics.

Although others before him had applied mathematics to physics, Boyle was one of the first to extend the application of mathematics to chemistry which he tried to develop as a science whose complex appearance was merely the result on simple mathematical laws applied to simple fundamental particles.

In 1668 Boyle left Oxford and went to live with his sister Lady Ranelagh in London. There he became a neighbour of Barrow but seemed to have more common scientific interests with another neighbour Thomas Sydenham, a physician. In 1669 his sister's husband died. Some however, were keen to find Boyle a wife. Wallis found someone whom he considered particularly suitable to be Boyle's wife and wrote to him saying:-

If I might be the happy instrument in making two so excellent persons happy in each other ... I do not know in what else I could more approve myself.

Boyle seemed to have successfully avoided such attempts to marry him off. In June 1670 he had a stroke which left him paralysed but slowly he recovered his health. He continued to work and to entertain at his London home. Visitors were so frequent that he had to restrict visits so that he had time to continue with his scientific researches, which he did with the help of many excellent assistants.

In 1680 he declined the offer that he serve as President of the Royal Society. He explained his reasons were religious in that he could not swear to necessary oaths. The religious side of Boyle is one which we have not mentioned in this biography, yet it was an important force in his life. Perhaps the reason it has not been necessary to mention his strong Christian faith earlier is that to Boyle there was no conflict with religion and a mechanistic world:-

... for him a God who could create a mechanical universe - who could create matter in motion, obeying certain laws out of which the universe as we know it could come into being in an orderly fashion - was far more to be admired and worshipped than a God who created a universe without scientific law.

Died: 30 Dec 1691 in London, England.

SIR C. V. RAMAN

Chandrasekhara Venkata Raman was born at Trichinopoly in Southern India on November 7th, 1888. His father was a lecturer in mathematics and physics so that from the first he was immersed in an academic atmosphere.

He entered Presidency College, Madras, in 1902, and in 1904 passed his B.A. examination, winning the first place and the gold medal in physics; in 1907 he gained his M.A. degree, obtaining the highest distinctions.

His earliest researches in optics and acoustics - the two fields of investigation to which he has dedicated his entire career - were carried out while he was a student.

Since at that time a scientific career did not appear to present the best possibilities, Raman joined the Indian Finance Department in 1907; though the duties of his office took most of his time, Raman found opportunities for carrying on experimental research in the laboratory of the Indian Association for the Cultivation of

Science at Calcutta (of which he became Honorary Secretary in 1919).

In 1917 he was offered the newly endowed Palit Chair of Physics at Calcutta University, and decided to accept it. After 15 years at Calcutta he became Professor at the Indian Institute of Science at Bangalore (1933-1948), and since 1948 he is Director of the Raman Institute of Research at Bangalore, established and endowed by himself. He also founded the *Indian Journal of Physics* in 1926, of which he is the Editor.

Raman sponsored the establishment of the Indian Academy of Sciences and has served as President since its inception. He also initiated the *Proceedings* of that academy, in which much of his work has been published, and is President of the Current Science Association, Bangalore, which publishes *Current Science (India).*

Some of Raman's early memoirs appeared as Bulletins of the *Indian Associationfor the Cultivation of Science* (Bull. 6 and 11, dealing with the "Maintenance of Vibrations"; Bull. 15, 1918, dealing with the theory of the musical instruments of the violin family). He contributed an article on the theory of musical instruments to the 8th Volume of the *Handbuch der Physik*, 1928.

In 1922 he published his work on the "Molecular Diffraction of Light", the first of a series of investigations with his collaborators which ultimately led to his discovery, on the 28th of February, 1928, of the radiation effect which bears his name ("A new radiation", *Indian J. Phys.*, 2 (1928) 387), and which gained him the 1930 Nobel Prize in Physics.

Other investigations carried out by Raman were: his experimental and theoretical studies on the diffraction of light by acoustic waves of ultrasonic and hypersonic frequencies (published 1934-1942), and those on the effects produced by X-rays on infrared vibrations in crystals exposed to ordinary light.

In 1948 Raman, through studying the spectroscopic behaviour of crystals, approached in a new manner fundamental problems of crystal dynamics. His laboratory has been dealing with the structure and properties of diamond, the structure and optical behaviour of numerous iridescent substances (labradorite, pearly felspar, agate, opal, and pearls).

Among his other interests have been the optics of colloids, electrical and magnetic anisotropy, and the physiology of human vision.

Raman has been honoured with a large number of honorary doctorates and memberships of scientific societies. He was elected a Fellow of the Royal Society early in his career (1924), and was knighted in 1929.

STEPHEN WILLIAM HAWKING

Stephen W. Hawking was born on January 8, 1942, in Oxford, England. His father, a well-known researcher in tropical medicine, urged his son to seek a career in the sciences. Stephen found biology and medicine too descriptive and lacking in exactness. Therefore, he turned to the study of mathematics and physics.

Hawking was not an outstanding student at St. Alban's School, Hertfordshire, nor later at Oxford University, which he entered in 1959. He was a sociable young man who did little schoolwork because he was able to grasp the essentials of a mathematics or physics problem quickly and intuitively.

While at Oxford he became increasingly interested in relativity theory and quantum mechanics, eventually graduating with a first class honors in physics (1962). He immediately began post-graduate studies at Cambridge University.

At Cambridge his talents were recognized by his major professor, the cosmologist Dennis W. Sciama, and he was encouraged to carry on his studies despite his growing physical disabilities. His marriage in 1965 to Jane Wilde was an important step in his emotional life.

Hawking made his first major contribution to science with his theorem of singularity, a work which grew out of his collaboration with theoretician Roger Penrose. A singularity is a place in either space or time at which some quantity becomes infinite. Such a place is found in a black hole, the final stage of a collapsed star, where the gravitational field has infinite strength. Penrose proved that a singularity was not a hypothetical construct; it could exist in the space-time of a real universe.

Hawking's research into the cosmological implications of singularities led him to study the properties of the best-known singularity: the black hole. Although a black hole is a discontinuity in space-time, its boundary, called the event horizon, can be detected. Hawking proved that the surface area of the event horizon of a black hole could only increase, not decrease, and that when two black holes merged the surface area of the new hole was larger than the sum of the two original surface areas.

Hawking's continuing examination of the nature of black holes led to two important discoveries. The first of them, that black holes can emit thermal radiation, was contrary to the claim that nothing could escape from a black hole. The second concerned the size of black holes. As originally conceived, black holes were immense in size because they were the end result of the collapse of gigantic stars.

Hawking summarized his scientific interests as "gravity—on all scales," from the realm of galaxies at one extreme to the subatomic at the other extreme. In the 1980s Hawking worked on a theory that Einstein unsuccessfully searched for in his later years.

As his physical condition grew worse Hawking's intellectual achievements increased. Not content with causing a revolution in cosmology, he presented a popular exposition of his ideas in *A Brief History of Time: From the Big Bang to Black Holes.* First published in 1988, this book acquired great popularity in the

United States. It sold over a million copies and was listed as the best-selling nonfiction book for over a year.

In 1993 Hawking wrote *Black Holes and Baby Universes and Other Essays,* which, in addition to a discussion of whether elementary particles that fall into black holes can form new, "baby" universes separate from our own, contains chapters about Hawking's personal life.

Hawking's work in modern cosmology and in theoretical astronomy and physics was widely recognized. He became a fellow of the Royal Society of London in 1974 and five years later was named to a professorial chair once held by Sir Isaac Newton: Lucasian professor of mathematics, Cambridge University. Beyond these honors he earned a host of honorary degrees, awards, prizes, and lectureships from the major universities and scientific societies of Europe and America.

These included the Eddington Medal of the Royal Astronomical Society, in 1975; the Pius XI Gold Medal, in 1975; the Maxwell Medal of the Institute of Physics, in 1976; the Albert Einstein Award of the Lewis and Rose Strauss Memorial Fund (the most prestigious award in theoretical physics), in 1978; the Franklin Medal of the Franklin Institute, in 1981; the Gold Medal of the Royal Society, in 1985; the Paul Dirac Medal and Prize, in 1987; and the Britannica Award, in 1989.

Hawking's endeavors include endorsing a wireless connection to the internet produced by U.S. Robotics Inc., beginning in March 1997, and speaking to wheelchair-bound youth. In addition, Hawking made an appearance on the television series *Star Trek*that his fans will not soon forget.

Hawking does not readily discuss his personal life, but it is generally know that he was divorced from his first wife in 1991 and they have two sons and a daughter.

SUBRAMANYAN CHANDRASEKHAR

Indian-born American astrophysicist who, with William A. Fowler, won the 1983 Nobel Prize for Physics for key discoveries that led to the currently accepted theory on the later evolutionary stages of massive stars.

Chandrasekhar was the nephew of Sir Chandrasekhara Venkata Raman, who won the Nobel Prize for Physics in 1930. Chandrasekhar was educated at Presidency College, at the University of Madras, and at Trinity College, Cambridge. From 1933 to 1936 he held a position at Trinity.

By the early 1930s, scientists had concluded that, after converting all of their hydrogen to helium, stars lose energy and contract under the influence of their own gravity.

These stars, known as white dwarf stars, contract to about the size of the Earth, and the electrons and nuclei of their constituent atoms are compressed to a state of extremely high density.

Chandrasekhar determined what is known as the Chandrasekhar limit—that a star having a mass more than 1.44 times that of the Sun does not form a white dwarf but instead continues to collapse, blows off its gaseous envelope in a supernova explosion, and becomes a neutron star.

Chandrasekhar joined the staff of the University of Chicago, rising from assistant professor of astrophysics (1938) to Morton D. Hull distinguished service professor of astrophysics (1952), and became a U.S. citizen in 1953.

He did important work on energy transfer by radiation in stellar atmospheres and convection on the solar surface. He also attempted to develop the mathematical theory of black holes, describing his work in *The Mathematical Theory of Black Holes* (1983).

Chandrasekhar was awarded the Gold Medal of the Royal Astronomical Society in 1953 and the Royal Medal of the Royal Society in 1962.

THE WRIGHT BROTHERS

The Wright brothers, Orville (August 19, 1871 – January 30, 1948) and Wilbur (April 16, 1867 – May 30, 1912), were two Americans who are generally credited with inventing and building the world's first successful airplane and making the first controlled, powered and sustained heavier-than-air human flight on December 17, 1903.

In the two years afterward, they developed their flying machine into the first practical fixed-wing aircraft. Although not the first to build and fly experimental aircraft, the Wright brothers were the first to invent aircraft controls that made mechanical fixed wing flight possible.

The brothers' fundamental breakthrough was their invention of "three axis-control," which enabled the pilot to steer the aircraft effectively and to maintain its equilibrium. This method became standard on fixed wing aircraft of all kinds. From the beginning of their aeronautical work, the Wright brothers focused on unlocking the secrets of control to conquer "the flying problem," rather than developing more powerful engines as some other experimenters did. Their U.S. patent 821,393 does not claim airplanes in general, but rather claims airplanes that are controlled by what were later termed ailerons.

Their careful wind tunnel tests produced better aeronautical data than any before, enabling them to design and build wings and propellers more effective than any before.

They gained the mechanical skills essential for their success by working for years in their shop with printing presses, bicycles, motors, and other machinery. Their work with bicycles in particular influenced their belief that an unstable vehicle like a flying machine could be controlled and balanced with practice.

The Wright brothers' status as inventors of the airplane has been subject to counter-claims by various parties. Much controversy persists over the many competing claims of early aviators.

The Wright brothers were two of seven children born to Milton Wright (1828–1917) and Susan Catherine Koerner (1831–1889). Wilbur Wright was born near Millville, Indiana in 1867; Orville in Dayton, Ohio in 1871.

The brothers never married. The other Wright siblings were named Reuchlin (1861–1920), Lorin (1862–1939), Katharine (1874–1929), and twins Otis and Ida (born 1870, died in infancy). In elementary school, Orville was given to mischief and was once expelled. In 1878 their father, who traveled often as a bishop in the Church of the United Brethren in Christ, brought home a toy "helicopter" for his two younger sons.

The device was based on an invention of French aeronautical pioneer Alphonse Penaud. Made of paper, bamboo and cork with a rubber band to twirl its rotor, it was about a foot long. Wilbur and Orville played with it until it broke, then built their own. In later years, they pointed to their experience with the toy as the initial spark of their interest in flying.

In the winter of 1885-86 Wilbur was accidentally struck in the face by a hockey stick while playing an ice-skating game with friends. He had been vigorous and athletic until then, and although his injuries did not appear especially severe, he became withdrawn, and did not attend Yale as planned. Had he enrolled, his career might have taken a very different path than the extraordinary one he eventually followed with Orville.

Instead, he spent the next few years largely housebound, caring for his mother who was terminally ill with tuberculosis and reading extensively in his father's library. He ably assisted his father during times of controversy within the Brethren Church. However, he also expressed unease over his own lack of ambition.

Both brothers received high school educations, but did not receive diplomas. The family's move in 1884 from Richmond, Indiana to Dayton (where the family had lived during the 1870s) prevented Wilbur from receiving his diploma after finishing four years of high school.

Orville dropped out after his junior year to start a printing business in 1889, having designed and built his own printing press with Wilbur's help. Quietly starting a partnership with far-reaching consequences, Wilbur joined the print shop, serving as editor while Orville was publisher of the weekly newspaper the *West Side News*, followed, for only a few months, by the daily *Evening Item*.

Capitalizing on the national bicycle craze, they opened a repair and sales shop in 1892 (the Wright Cycle Exchange, later the Wright Cycle Company) and began manufacturing their own brand in 1896. They used this endeavor to fund their growing interest in flight. In the early or mid-1890s they saw newspaper or magazine articles and probably photographs of the dramatic glides by Otto Lilienthal in Germany.

The year 1896 brought three important aeronautical events. In May, Smithsonian Institution Secretary Samuel Langley successfully flew an unmanned steam-powered model aircraft. In the summer, Chicago engineer and aviation authority Octave Chanute brought together several men who tested various types of gliders over the sand dunes along the shore of Lake Michigan.

In August, Lilienthal was killed in the plunge of his glider. These events lodged in the consciousness of the brothers. In May 1899 Wilbur wrote a letter to the Smithsonian Institution requesting information and publications about aeronautics. Drawing on the work of Sir George Cayley, Chanute, Lilienthal, Leonardo da Vinci, and Langley, they began their mechanical aeronautical experimentation that year.

The Wright brothers always presented a unified image to the public, sharing equally in the credit for their invention. Biographers note, however, that Wilbur took the initiative in 1899–1900, writing of "my" machine and "my" plans before Orville became deeply involved when the first person singular became the plural "we" and "our".

Author James Tobin asserts, "it is impossible to imagine Orville, bright as he was, supplying the driving force that started their work and kept it going from the back room of a store in Ohio to conferences with capitalists, presidents, and kings. Will did that. He was the leader, from the beginning to the end."

The Wrights did all the theoretical work and most of the hands-on construction. Their bicycle shop employee Charlie Taylor became an important part of the team, building their first aircraft engine in close collaboration with the brothers.

Despite Lilienthal's fate, the brothers favored his strategy: to practice gliding in order to master the art of control before attempting motor-driven flight.

The death of British aeronaut Percy Pilcher in another hang gliding crash in 1899 only reinforced their opinion that a reliable method of pilot control was the key to successful—and safe—flight. At the outset of their experiments they regarded control as the unsolved third part of "the flying problem".

They believed sufficiently promising knowledge of the other two issues—wings and engines—already existed. The Wright brothers thus differed sharply from more experienced practitioners of the day, notably Ader, Maxim and Langley who built powerful engines, attached them to airframes equipped with unproven control devices, and expected to take to the air with no previous flying experience. Though agreeing with Lilienthal's idea of practice, the Wrights saw that his method of balance and control—shifting his body weight—was fatally inadequate. They were determined to find something better.

Based on obsevation, Wilbur concluded that birds changed the angle of the ends of their wings to make their bodies roll right or left. The brothers decided this would also be a good way for a flying machine to turn—to "bank" or "lean" into the turn just like a bird—and just like a person riding a bicycle, an experience with which they were thoroughly familiar.

Equally important, they hoped this method would enable recovery when the wind tilted the machine to one side (lateral balance). They puzzled over how to achieve the same effect with man-made wings and eventually discovered wing-warping when Wilbur idly twisted a long inner tube box at the bicycle shop.

Other aeronautical investigators regarded flight as if it were not so different from surface locomotion, except the surface would be elevated. They thought in terms of a ship's rudder for steering, while the flying machine remained essentially level in the air, as did a train or an automobile or a ship at the surface.

The idea of deliberately leaning, or rolling, to one side either seemed undesirable or did not enter their thinking. Some of these other investigators, including Langley and Chanute, sought the elusive ideal of "inherent stability," believing the pilot of a flying machine would not be able to react quickly enough to wind disturbances to use mechanical controls effectively.

The Wright brothers, on the other hand, wanted the pilot to have absolute control. For that reason, their early designs made no concessions toward built-in stability (such as dihedral wings). They deliberately designed their 1903 first powered flyer with anhedral (drooping) wings, which are inherently unstable, but less susceptible to upset by gusty sidewinds.

Toward flight: In July 1899 Wilbur put wing-warping to the test by building and flying a five-foot box kite in the approximate shape of a biplane. When the wings were warped, or twisted, one end would receive more lift and rise, starting a turn in the direction of the lower end. Warping was controlled by four lines attached to the kite. The lines led to two sticks held by the kite flyer, who tilted them in opposite directions to twist the wings and make the kite bank left or right. It worked.

In 1900 the brothers journeyed to Kitty Hawk, North Carolina to begin their manned gliding experiments. They chose the location based on advice from Octave Chanute (answering Wilbur's letter), who suggested a sandy coastal area for regular breezes and a soft landing surface. They selected Kitty Hawk after scrutinizing Weather Bureau data and writing to the government meteorologist stationed there.

The location, although remote, was closer to Dayton than other places Chanute had suggested, including California and Florida. The spot also gave them privacy from reporters, who had turned the 1896 Chanute experiments at Lake Michigan into something of a circus.

The trip required a train ride from Dayton to Cincinnati; change trains for an overnight ride to Old Point Comfort, Virginia (near Newport News); ferryboat to Norfolk; train to Elizabeth City, North Carolina; and boat ride to Kitty Hawk on the Outer Banks of North Carolina.

The gliders : They based the design of their first full-size glider on the work of their recent predecessors: the Chanute-Herring "double-decker," a biplane hang glider which flew well in the 1896 experiments near Chicago; and aeronautical data on lift that Lilienthal had published.

The uprights between the wings of their glider were braced by wires in their own adaptation of Chanute's modified "Pratt truss," a bridge-building design he applied to his 1896 glider. The Wrights mounted the horizontal elevator in front of the wings rather than behind, apparently believing this feature would help avoid a nosedive and crash like the one that killed Lilienthal. (Later, when Santos-Dumont flew his *14-bis* in Paris in 1906, the French dubbed the tail-first arrangement a "canard," due to the supposed resemblance to a duck in flight.)

According to some Wright biographers, Wilbur probably did all the gliding until 1902, perhaps to exercise his authority as older brother and to protect Orville from harm.

1900 Glider :The brothers flew the glider only a few days in the early autumn of 1900 at Kitty Hawk. In the first tests, probably Oct. 3, Wilbur was aboard while the glider flew as a kite not far above the ground with men below holding tether ropes. Most of the kite tests were unpiloted with sandbags or chains (and even a local boy) as onboard ballast.

They tested wing-warping using control ropes from the ground. The glider was also tested unmanned while suspended from a small homemade tower. Wilbur (but not Orville) made about a dozen free glides on only a single day. For those tests, the brothers trekked four miles (6 km) south to the Kill Devil Hills, a group of sand dunes up to 100 feet (30 m) high (where they made camp in each of the next three years).

Although the glider's lift was less than expected (causing most tests to be unmanned), the brothers were encouraged because the craft's front elevator worked well and they had no accidents. However, the small number of free glides meant they were not able to give wing-warping a true test.

The pilot lay flat on the lower wing, as planned, to reduce aerodynamic drag. As a glide ended, the pilot was supposed to lower himself to a vertical position through an opening in the wing and land on his feet with his arms wrapped over the framework.

Within a few glides, however, they discovered the pilot could remain prone on the wing, headfirst, without undue danger when landing. They made all their flights in that position for the next five years.

1901 Glider : Hoping to improve lift, they built the 1901 glider with a much larger wing area and made 50 to 100 flights in July and August for distances of 20 to 400 feet (120 m). The glider stalled a few times, but the parachute effect of the forward elevator allowed Wilbur to make a safe flat or "pancake" landing, instead of a nose-dive.

These incidents wedded the Wrights even more strongly to the *canard* design, which they did not give up until 1910. The glider, however, delivered two major disappointments.

It produced only about one-third the lift calculated and sometimes failed to respond properly to wing-warping, turning opposite the direction intended—a problem later known as adverse yaw.

On the trip home after their second season, Wilbur, stung with disappointment, remarked to Orville that man would fly, but not in their lifetimes.

In 1903, the brothers built the powered Wright Flyer I, using their preferred material for construction, spruce, a strong and lightweight wood. They also designed and carved their own wooden propellers, and had a purpose-built gasoline engine fabricated in their bicycle shop.

They thought propeller design would be a simple matter and intended to adapt data from shipbuilding. However, their library research disclosed no established formulas for either marine or air propellers, and they found themselves with no sure starting point.

They discussed and argued the question, sometimes heatedly, until they concluded that an aeronautical propeller is essentially a wing rotating in the vertical plane.

On that basis, they used data from more wind tunnel tests to design their propellers. The finished blades were just over eight feet long, made of three laminations of glued spruce.

The Wrights decided on twin "pusher" propellers (counter-rotating to cancel torque), which would act on a greater quantity of air than a single relatively slow propeller and not disturb airflow over the leading edge of the wings.

Wilbur made a March 1903 entry in his notebook indicating the prototype propeller was 66% efficient. Modern wind tunnel tests on reproduction 1903 propellers show they were more than 75% efficient under the conditions of the first flights, and actually had a peak efficiency of 82%. This is a remarkable achievement, considering that modern wooden propellers have a maximum efficiency of 85%.

The Wrights wrote to several engine manufacturers, but none met their need for a sufficiently lightweight powerplant. They turned to their talented shop mechanic, Charlie Taylor (a largely unsung hero of the Wright aviation era), who built an engine in just six weeks in close consultation with the brothers.

To keep the weight low enough, the engine block was cast from aluminum, a rare practice for the time. The Wright/Taylor engine was a primitive version of modern fuel-injection systems, having no carburetor or fuel pump. Gasoline was gravity-fed into the crankcase through a rubber tube from the fuel tank mounted on a wing strut.

The propeller drive chains, resembling those of bicycles, were actually supplied by a manufacturer of heavy-duty automobile chain-drives. The *Flyer* cost less than a thousand dollars to construct. It had a wingspan of 40 feet (12 m), weighed 625 pounds (283 kg), and sported a 12 hp (9 kW), 170 pound (77 kg) engine.

After weeks of delays at Kitty Hawk caused by broken propeller shafts during engine tests, Wilbur won a coin toss and made a three-second flight attempt on December 14, 1903, stalling after takeoff and causing minor damage to the Flyer.

In a message to their family, Wilbur referred to the trial as having "only partial success", stating "the power is ample, and but for a trifling error due to lack of experience with this machine and this method of starting, the machine would undoubtedly have flown beautifully." Following repairs, the Wrights finally took to the air on December 17, 1903, making two flights each from level ground into a freezing headwind gusting to 27 miles (43 km) an hour.

The first flight, by Orville, of 120 feet (36.5 m) in 12 seconds, at a speed of only 6.8 mph over the ground, was recorded in a famous photograph. The next two flights covered approximately 175 and 200 feet (60 m), by Wilbur and Orville respectively. Their altitude was about ten feet above the ground. Here is Orville Wright's account of the final flight of the day:

Wilbur started the fourth and last flight at just about 12 o'clock. The first few hundred feet were up and down, as before, but by the time three hundred feet had been covered, the machine was under much better control. The course for the next four or five hundred feet had but little undulation. However, when out about eight hundred feet the machine began pitching again, and, in one of its darts downward, struck the ground.

The distance over the ground was measured to be 852 feet (260 m); the time of the flight was 59 seconds. The frame supporting the front rudder was badly broken, but the main part of the machine was not injured at all. We estimated that the machine could be put in condition for flight again in about a day or two.

The flights were witnessed by five people: Adam Etheridge, John Daniels and Will Dough of the coastal lifesaving crew; area businessman W.C. Brinkley; and Johnny Moore, a boy from the village, making these arguably the first public flights. A telegraph operator relaying a message to their father leaked the news against the brothers' wishes, and highly inaccurate reports ran in several newspapers the next day.

After the men hauled the Flyer back from its fourth flight, a powerful gust of wind flipped it over several times, despite the crew's attempt to hold it down. Severely damaged, the airplane never flew again. The brothers shipped it home, and years later Orville restored it, lending it to several U.S. locations for display, then to a British museum (see Smithsonian dispute below), before it was finally installed in the Smithsonian Institution in Washington, D.C. in 1948.

In 1904 the brothers built the *Flyer II* and set up an airfield at Huffman Prairie, a cow pasture eight miles (13 km) northeast of Dayton which bank president Torrance Huffman let them use rent-free. They invited reporters to their first flight attempt of the year on May 23 on the condition that no photographs be taken.

Engine troubles and slack winds prevented any flying, and they could manage only a very short hop a few days later with fewer reporters present.

Some scholars of the Wrights speculate the brothers may have intentionally failed to fly in order to disinterest reporters in their experiments. Whether that is true is not known, but after their poor showing local newspapers virtually ignored them for the next year and a half.

The Wrights were glad to be free from the distraction of reporters. The absence of newsmen also reduced the chance of competitors learning their methods.

After the Kitty Hawk powered flights, the Wrights made a decision to begin withdrawing from the bicycle business so they could devote themselves to creating and marketing a practical airplane.

The decision was financially risky, since they were neither wealthy nor government-funded (unlike other experimenters such as Ader, Maxim, Langley and Santos-Dumont). They did not have the luxury of giving away their invention; it was to be their livelihood. Thus, their secrecy intensified, encouraged by advice from their patent attorney not to reveal details of their machine.

At Huffman Prairie, lighter winds and lower air density than in Kitty Hawk (due to Ohio's higher altitude and higher temperatures) made takeoffs very difficult, and they had to use a much longer starting rail, stretching to hundreds of feet, compared to the 60-foot (18 m) rail at Kitty Hawk.

During the spring and summer they suffered many hard landings, real crackups, repeated Flyer damage, and bodily bumps and bruises.

On August 13, making an unassisted takeoff, Wilbur finally exceeded their best Kitty Hawk effort with a flight of 1,300 feet (400 m). Then they decided to use a weight-powered catapult to make takeoffs easier and tried it for the first time on September 7. On September 20, 1904 Wilbur flew the first complete circle in history by a manned heavier-than-air powered machine, covering 4,080 feet (1,244 m) in about a minute and a half.

Their two best flights were November 9 by Wilbur and December 1 by Orville, each exceeding five minutes and covering about three miles in almost four circles.

By the end of the year the brothers had accumulated about 50 minutes in the air in 105 flights over the rather soggy 85 acre pasture, which, remarkably, is virtually unchanged today from its original condition and is now part of Dayton Aviation Heritage National Historical Park, adjacent to Wright-Patterson Air Force Base.

The Wright brothers were certainly complicit in the lack of attention they received. Wary of the competition stealing their plans, after 1905 they refused to make public flights or take part in air shows unless they had a firm contract to sell their airplane.

They attempted to interest the military in the U.S., France, Britain, and Germany, but were rebuffed because they insisted on a signed contract before giving a demonstration.

American bureaucrats, having recently spent $50,000 on the Langley Aerodrome—a product of the nation's foremost scientist—only to see it plunge twice into the Potomac River "like a handful of mortar," were particularly unreceptive to the claims of two unknown bicycle makers from Ohio.

Thus, doubted or scorned, the Wright brothers continued their work in semi-obscurity, while other aviation pioneers like Brazilian Alberto Santos-Dumont and American Glenn Curtiss entered the limelight.

The Wright brothers made no flights at all in 1906 and 1907 while they pursued fitful negotiations with the U.S. and European governments. After finally signing contracts with a French company and the U.S. Army, they went back to Kitty Hawk in May 1908 with the 1905 Flyer, modified with seats for pilot and passenger, and began practicing for their all-important demonstration flights.

Their contracts required them to be able to carry a passenger. After tests with sandbags in the passenger seat, Charlie Furnas, a helper from Dayton, became the first fixed-wing aircraft passenger on a few short flights May 14. For safety, and as a promise to their father, Wilbur and Orville did not fly together.

THOMAS EDISON

Thomas Alva Edison was born on February 11, 1847 in Milan, Ohio; the seventh and last child of Samuel and Nancy Edison. When Edison was seven his family moved to Port Huron, Michigan. Edison lived here until he struck out on his own at the age of sixteen. Edison had very little formal education as a child, attending school only for a few months.

He was taught reading, writing, and arithmetic by his mother, but was always a very curious child and taught himself much by reading on his own. This belief in self-improvement remained throughout his life.

Edison began working at an early age, as most boys did at the time. At thirteen he took a job as a newsboy, selling newspapers and candy on the local railroad that ran through Port Huron to Detroit.

He seems to have spent much of his free time reading scientific, and technical books, and also had the opportunity at this time to learn how to operate a telegraph. By the time he was sixteen, Edison was proficient enough to work as a telegrapher full time. The development of the telegraph was the first step in the communication revolution, and the telegraph industry expanded rapidly in the second half of the 19th century.

This rapid growth gave Edison and others like him a chance to travel, see the country, and gain experience. Edison worked in a number of cities throughout the United States before arriving in Boston in 1868. Here Edison began to change his profession from telegrapher to inventor.

He received his first patent on an electric vote recorder, a device intended for use by elected bodies such as Congress to speed the voting process. This invention was a commercial failure. Edison resolved that in the future he would only invent things that he was certain the public would want.

Edison moved to New York City in 1869. He continued to work on inventions related to the telegraph, and developed his first successful invention, an improved stock ticker called the "Universal Stock Printer". For this and some related inventions Edison was paid $40,000.

This gave Edison the money he needed to set up his first small laboratory and manufacturing facility in Newark, New Jersey in 1871. During the next five years, Edison worked in Newark inventing and manufacturing devices that greatly improved the speed and efficiency of the telegraph. He also found to time to get married to Mary Stilwell and start a family.

In 1876 Edison sold all his Newark manufacturing concerns and moved his family and staff of assistants to the small village of Menlo Park, twenty-five miles southwest of New York City.

Edison established a new facility containing all the equipment necessary to work on any invention. This research and development laboratory was the first of its kind anywhere; the model for later, modern facilities such as Bell Laboratories, this is sometimes considered to be Edison's greatest invention. Here

Edison began to change the world. The first great invention developed by Edison in Menlo Park was the tin foil phonograph. The first machine that could record and reproduce sound created a sensation and brought Edison international fame. Edison toured the country with the tin foil phonograph, and was invited to the White House to demonstrate it to President Rutherford B. Hayes in April 1878.

Edison next undertook his greatest challenge, the development of a practical incandescent, electric light. The idea of electric lighting was not new, and a number of people had worked on, and even developed forms of electric lighting. But up to that time, nothing had been developed that was remotely practical for home use.

Edison's eventual achievement was inventing not just an incandescent electric light, but also an electric lighting system that contained all the elements necessary to make the incandescent light practical, safe, and economical.

After one and a half years of work, success was achieved when an incandescent lamp with a filament of carbonized sewing thread burned for thirteen and a half hours. The first public demonstration of the Edison's incandescent lighting system was in December 1879, when the Menlo Park laboratory complex was electrically lighted. Edison spent the next several years creating the electric industry.

In September 1882, the first commercial power station, located on Pearl Street in lower Manhattan, went into operation providing light and power to customers in a one square mile area; the electric age had begun.

The success of his electric light brought Edison to new heights of fame and wealth, as electricity spread around the world. Edison's various electric companies continued to grow until in 1889 they were brought together to form Edison General Electric.

Despite the use of Edison in the company title however, Edison never controlled this company. The tremendous amount of capital needed to develop the incandescent lighting industry had necessitated the involvement of investment bankers such as J.P. Morgan. When Edison General Electric merged with its leading competitor Thompson-Houston in 1892, Edison was dropped from the name, and the company became simply General Electric. This period of success was marred by the death of Edison's wife Mary in 1884.

Edison's involvement in the business end of the electric industry had caused Edison to spend less time in Menlo Park. After Mary's death, Edison was there even less, living instead in New York City with his three children. A year later, while vacationing at a friends house in New England, Edison met Mina Miller and fell in love.

The couple was married in February 1886 and moved to West Orange, New Jersey where Edison had purchased an estate, Glenmont, for his bride. Thomas Edison lived here with Mina until his death.

When Edison moved to West Orange, he was doing experimental work in makeshift facilities in his electric lamp factory in nearby Harrison, New Jersey. A few months after his marriage, however, Edison decided to build a new laboratory in West Orange itself, less than a mile from his home.

Edison possessed the both the resources and experience by this time to build, "the best equipped and largest laboratory extant and the facilities superior to any other for rapid and cheap development of an invention". The new laboratory complex consisting of five buildings opened in November 1887.

A three story main laboratory building contained a power plant, machine shops, stock rooms, experimental rooms and a large library. Four smaller one story buildings built perpendicular to the main building contained a physics lab, chemistry lab, metallurgy lab, pattern shop, and chemical storage.

The large size of the laboratory not only allowed Edison to work on any sort of project, but also allowed him to work on as many as ten or twenty projects at once. Facilities were added to the laboratory or modified to meet Edison's changing needs as he continued to work in this complex until his death in 1931. Over the years, factories to manufacture Edison inventions were built around the laboratory.

The entire laboratory and factory complex eventually covered more than twenty acres and employed 10,000 people at its peak during World War One (1914-1918). After opening the new laboratory, Edison began to work on the phonograph again, having set the project aside to develop the electric light in the late 1870s.

By the 1890s, Edison began to manufacture phonographs for both home, and business use. Like the electric light, Edison developed everything needed to have a phonograph work, including records to play, equipment to record the records, and equipment to manufacture the records and the machines.

In the process of making the phonograph practical, Edison created the recording industry. The development and improvement of the phonograph was an ongoing project, continuing almost until Edison's death.

VIKRAM SARABHAI

Considered the Father of the Indian space program; instrumental in establishing the Physical Research Laboratory (PRL) in Ahmedabad in November 1947; was Chairman of the Atomic Energy Commission. He along with other Ahmedabad-based industrialists played a major role in the creation of the Indian Institute of Management, Ahmedabad.

Vikram Sarabhai was one of the greatest scientists of India. He is considered as the Father of the Indian space program. Apart from being a scientist, he was a rare combination of an innovator, industrialist and visionary.

Vikram Ambalal Sarabhai was born on August 12, 1919 at Ahmedabad in an affluent family of progressive industrialists. He was one of eight children of Ambalal and Sarla Devi. He had his early education in a private school, "Retreat" run by his parents on Montessori lines. Some of the great men of India such as Gurudev Rabindranath, J. Krishna Murthi, Motilal Nehru, V. S.

Shrinivasa Shastri, Jawaharlal Nehru, Sarojini Naidu, Maulana Azad, C. F. Andrews, C. V. Raman et al. used to stay with the Sarabhai family when they visited Ahmedabad. Mahatma Gandhi also once stayed at their house while recovering from an illness. Visits by such great men greatly influenced Vikram Sarabhai.

After his matriculation, Vikram Sarabhai proceeded to Cambridge for his college education and took the tripods degree from St. John's college in 1940. When World War II began, he returned home and joined as a research scholar under Sir C. V. Raman at the Indian Institute of Science, Bangalore His interest in solar physics and cosmic ray led him to set up many observation stations around the country.

He built the necessary equipment with which he took measurements at Bangalore, Poona and the Himalayas. He returned to Cambridge in 1945 and completed his Ph.D in 1947.

Vikram Sarabhai was instrumental in establishing the Physical Research Laboratory (PRL) in Ahmedabad in November 1947. The laboratory was established in a few rooms in M.G. Science Institute of the Ahmedabad Education Society, which was founded by his parents. Subsequently, it got support from the Council of Scientific and Industrial Research (CSIR) and the Department of Atomic Energy.

Vikram Sarabhai did research on the time variations of cosmic rays and concluded that meteorological effects could not entirely affect the observed daily variations of cosmic rays; further, the residual variations were wide and global and these were related to variations in solar activity. Vikram Sarabhai visualized a new field of research opening up in solar and interplanetary Physics.

The year 1957-1958 was designated as International Geo-physical year (IGY). The Indian program for the IGY had been one of the most significant ventures of Sarabhai. It exposed him to the new vistas of space science with the launching in 1957 of Sputnik-I. Subsequently, the Indian National Committee for Space Research was created, of which Vikram Sarabhai became Chairman.

With active support from Homi Bhabha, Vikram Sarabhai, set up the first Rocket Launching station (TERLS) in the country at Thumba near Thiruvananthapuram on the Arabian Coast, as Thumba is very close to the Equator. The first rocket with sodium vapour payload was launched on November 21, 1963. In 1965, the UN General Assembly gave recognition to TERLS as an international facility.

After the sudden death of Homi Bhabha in an air crash, Vikram Sarabhai was appointed Chairman, Atomic Energy Commission in May 1966. He wanted the practical application of science to reach the common man. He decided to acquire competence in advance technology for the solution of country's problems based on technical and economic evaluation of its real resources. He initiated India's space programme, which today is renowned all over the world.

Dr. Vikram Sarabhai was awarded with Shanti Swarup Bhatnagar Medal in 1962 and Padma Bhushan in 1966. Vikram Sarabhai passed away in his sleep on December 31,1971.

VENKATRAMAN RAMAKRISHNAN

Venkatraman "Venki" Ramakrishnan (born: 1952) is an Indian-born American and British structural biologist, who shared the 2009 Nobel Prize in Chemistry with Thomas A. Steitz and Ada E. Yonath, "for studies of the structure and function of the ribosome". Since 1999, he has worked as a group leader at the Medical Research Council (MRC) Laboratory of Molecular Biology (LMB) on the Cambridge Biomedical Campus, UK and is a Fellow of Trinity College, Cambridge. He served as President of the Royal Society from 2015 to 2020.

Ramakrishnan was born in Chidambaram in Cuddalore district of Tamil Nadu, India to C. V. Ramakrishnan and Rajalakshmi. Both his parents were scientists and taught biochemistry at the Maharaja Sayajirao University in Baroda.

He moved to Vadodara (previously also known as Baroda) in Gujarat at the age of three, where he had his schooling at Convent of Jesus and Mary, except for spending 1960–61 in Adelaide, Australia.

Following his Pre-Science at the Maharaja Sayajirao University of Baroda, he did his undergraduate studies in the same university on a National Science Talent Scholarship, graduating with a BSc degree in Physics in 1971.

In a January 2010 lecture at the Indian Institute of Science, he revealed that he failed to get admitted to any of the Indian Institutes of Technology or the Christian Medical College, Vellore, Tamil Nadu.

Immediately after graduation he moved to the U.S.A., where he obtained his PhD degree in Physics from Ohio University in 1976. He then spent two years studying biology as a graduate student at the University of California, San Diego while making a transition from theoretical physics to biology.

Ramakrishnan began work on ribosomes as a postdoctoral fellow with Peter Moore at Yale University. After his post-doctoral fellowship, he initially could not find a faculty position even though he had applied to about 50 universities in the U.S.

He continued to work on ribosomes from 1983-95 as a staff scientist at Brookhaven National Laboratory. In 1995 he moved to the University of Utah as a Professor of Biochemistry, and in 1999, he moved to his current position at the Medical Research Council Laboratory of Molecular Biology in Cambridge, England, where he had also been a sabbatical visitor during 1991-92.

In 1999, Ramakrishnan's laboratory published a 5.5 Angstrom resolution structure of the 30S subunit. The following year, his laboratory determined the complete molecular structure of the 30S subunit of the ribosome and its complexes with several antibiotics.

This was followed by studies that provided structural insights into the mechanism that ensures the fidelity of protein biosynthesis.

More recently, his laboratory has determined the atomic structure of the whole ribosome in complex with its tRNA and mRNA ligands. Ramakrishnan is also known for his past work on histone and chromatin structure.

Ramakrishnan is a Fellow of the Royal Society, a member of EMBO and the U.S. National Academy of Sciences and a Fellow of Trinity College, Cambridge. He was awarded the 2007 Louis-Jeantet Prize for Medicine, the 2008 Heatley Medal of the British Biochemical Society and the 2009 Rolf-Sammet Professorship at the Goethe University Frankfurt.

In 2009, Ramakrishnan was awarded the Nobel Prize in Chemistry along with Thomas A. Steitz and Ada Yonath. He received India's second highest civilian honor, the Padma Vibhushan, in 2010.

Ramakrishnan was knighted in the 2012 New Year Honours for services to Molecular Biology, but does not generally use the title.

Ramakrishnan is married to Vera Rosenberry, an author and illustrator of children's books. His stepdaughter Tanya Kapka is a doctor in Oregon, and his son Raman Ramakrishnan is a cellist based in New York.

~~~
~~~